To John, of course, and
to other young prospects
with and without middle names

and the Pineapple Cheesecake Scare

Sands Hetherington

Illustrations by Jessica Love

DUNE BUGGY PRESS
Greensboro, NC

Night Buddies
and the Pineapple Cheesecake Scare

By Sands Hetherington

Illustrations by Jessica Love

Published by:
Dune Buggy Press
3 Deerwood Court, Greensboro, NC 27410
www.dunebuggypress.com

Text copyright © 2012 by Sands Hetherington
Illustrations copyright © 2012 by Jessica Love

ISBN: 978-0-9847417-1-7
Library of Congress Control Number: 2011942720

Publisher's Cataloging-In-Publication Data
(Prepared by The Donohue Group, Inc.)

Hetherington, Sands.
 Night buddies and the pineapple cheesecake scare / Sands Hetherington ; illustrations by Jessica Love.

 p. : ill. ; cm. -- (Night buddies ; Bk. 1)

 Previously published: Night buddies. Pittsburgh, PA : Dorrance Publishing Co., 2000.
 Summary: John Degraffenreidt and his new friend, Crosley, a zany red crocodile, get to know each other better as they travel to the Cheesecake Factory to save the world's supply of pineapple cheesecakes.
 Interest age group: 007-009.
 ISBN: 978-0-9847417-1-7

 1. Crocodiles--Juvenile fiction. 2. Cheesecake--Juvenile fiction. 3. Crocodiles--Fiction. 4. Cake--Fiction. 5. Fantasy fiction. 6. Adventure stories. I. Love, Jessica. II. Title.

PZ7.H28 Nig 2012
[Fic]   2011942720

Editor: Gail M. Kearns, www.topressandbeyond.com
Book and cover design: Peri Poloni-Gabriel, www.knockoutbooks.com
Cover and interior illustrations: Jessica Love, www.jessicalove.org
Book production coordinated by To Press & Beyond

Printed in the United States of America

Night Buddies
Uncommon Words

CROSLEY SPEAK

Yerk! Yerk!: (Laughing) Ha! Ha!

Jeeks!: Gosh!; Golly!; Gee whiz!

Har?: (Questioning) What?; Huh?

Yigg!: Oh no!; Rats!

Excelsior!: Totally super!

Blorf!: A snorting noise, often of frustration

Shnorf!: See Blorf!

Wuff!: Gasping for air

Snerk!: Alarm or chagrin

IGUANA LINGO

Hig! Hig!: See Yerk! Yerk!

Soo-Wee!: Man, is that ever nauseating!

CRENWINKLE LANGUAGE

Fraternally: Brother-to-brother

GENERAL

Whatchamacallit: A small object having a special power and suitable for hanging on Crosley's belt.

CHAPTER ONE

My name's John Degraffenreidt and I'm a kid and this is about me and Cros and —— okay, there's lots of others too, but Cros and me are the featured guys, right?

I didn't want to go to bed is how the whole thing got started. It's why the Night Buddies got in it too, but don't worry, you'll find all that out. Just make sure you know that I really did put up this huge fuss.

I wouldn't brush my teeth, right? And I didn't want to take my clothes off. I argued about everything in the world for several minutes. And when I finally did get in bed, I threw the covers off and sat straight up.

"I'm real hungry," I yapped at Mom and Dad.

Dad grinned and tried to cover me back up. "How can you be hungry? You ate so much pineapple cheesecake I thought you'd get sick." Then Mom kissed me on top of my head where it's real curly and clicked off the light and they went away.

"But I wanted some more!" I yelled after them.

"Sleep tight," Mom said from somewhere. "Love you."

"My belly hurts!" I hollered in the dark, but I knew it wouldn't do any good.

And it didn't either. So in a minute I rolled over and shut my eyes. "I *did* want some more," I fussed, and then I pulled the covers up around my ears.

"Funny ya should mention pineapple cheesecakes tonight," said the sound. **CLACK!** *"Hey, I wonder if any's left."*

It sounded like a whole lot of rocks scraping together. And sometimes like a big mousetrap trapping —— **CLACK!** —— There, it did it again and made the bed jump. It came from down on the floor, and I scooted to the edge of the bed and looked over.

There was a light beam squirting out from underneath.

"I'm King o' the Hogs about pineapple cheesecakes!

YERK! YERK! YERK! YERK!"

The light beam bobbed around some more, and then a flashlight poked out, the regular kind like you get in drugstores. A scaly foot with big ol' claws was holding it!

I watched and waited. I wasn't scared, I mean not exactly. I couldn't think of any reason to be scared. And like I said, I wasn't ready to go to bed yet anyway.

The scaly foot holding the flashlight was connected to a short lumpy leg, and right after that, edging out sideways from underneath and shoving two video games and my catcher's mitt out first, was the rest of a fairly regular-looking crocodile in a bright yellow suit. Fairly regular-looking except for one thing: as soon as the flashlight flashed on his hide, I could see that he was red. Red as red paint.

So this character gets up and straightens his suit out and sits down in my chair. It was a funny sight, too. His stubby back legs stuck straight out in front, and his giant tail went down the side of the chair and all the way around it on the floor. But he did it easy enough, like he had sat in all sorts of chairs. He folded his stumpy front legs across his chest and blinked at me.

"Well, little buddy, what d'ya know, here I am! I'll tell ya somethin' else too. This business about squeezin' under beds is gettin' tiresome. What would ya say if I was t' start —— Awright," he pointed, "like hidin' in that closet right over there?"

"Fine with me," I blinked back. "You said you were a hog, though. You sure don't look like one too much."

"Now why would I wanna be one o' them guys? Hogs make dumb-lookin' crocodiles," he said. "Ain't *that* a fact!" **CLACK! CLACK!**

This was his two zillion teeth clacking together. I figured he must like the sound of it. He grinned at me with about one zillion: "What I meant was, I act like a hog when I eat pineapple cheesecakes. I can't hardly stop."

"Hey, me too," I grinned, kicking off my covers. I decided he sounded more like a chain saw than anything else. One with the volume knob turned down.

"It's just weird it should come up right now," said the crocodile. And he stopped and blinked again. "I mean here I sit, your brand-new Night Buddy, first time on the job, an' the very first thing anybody talks about is pineapple cheesecakes! **YERK! YERK! YERK!**"

He laughed and turned his feet bottoms-up like when you ask a question: "Jeeks, little buddy, that's the whole *Program* for tonight. That's what we're gonna go *see* about. The big factory where they make all the pineapple cheesecakes in the world, over across the river, it turns out they're in a whole lotta trouble, an' we gotta go over an' try an' *help* 'em."

I sat up on the edge of the bed: "Try an' help 'em what?"

"Help 'em any which way we can," said the crocodile. "They ain't shipped a single pineapple cheesecake since the trouble started way last week. An' pretty soon there ain't gonna *be* any pineapple cheesecakes. Nowhere anyplace, little buddy! **JEEKS!**"

I kicked my heel at the bottom of the bed: "I'm not little."

"Har?" said the crocodile.

"I'm not little," I said. "You keep callin' me little."

"**YIGG!** Hey, I sure didn't mean t' make ya sore. Sure didn't mean t' do *that*. No *sir*. It's just —— That's what we usually say in the Night Buddies." He blinked six or seven times. "So okay, what d'ya guess we oughta call ya, then? What d'ya think?"

"Everybody I know calls me John," I said, and kicked the bed again.

"Well awright," said the crocodile. "Sure, we'll call ya John."

"It's the name I got born with."

"An' hey!" he said. "It's a super name, too, ain't it? That sure is a super name or my name's Mary Poppins." He rattled this big bunch of little whatchamacallits he had hanging on his belt: "I'm Crosley, by the way. I ain't really Mary Poppins."

"Crosley?" I had to giggle. "Hey, that's cool! Crosley Crocodile, I like that."

"YERK! YERK! Yeah, it's just Crosley, though. That's all the name I need."

I pulled on a curl on the top of my head like I do a lot: "Just Crosley?"

Crosley nodded: "Sure, buddy. Ya can awready see I'm a crocodile, right?"

"Boy, I sure can."

"So why do I need t' bark it around, huh? Whatta I need another name for, long as everybody can see?"

"I guess that makes sense," I said. "But ya know what? When ya meet somebody you're supposed t' shake hands with 'em."

"Well I'll just belch, John. That's exackly what *I* was gonna suggest. Put 'er there, buddy —— "

And he hopped off the chair quick like a bird and held his front foot out. I got up and shook the foot, claws and all. Then he sat back down and flashed his flashlight around the room. He flashed it on my chest of drawers. "Okay," he said. "Time t' get dressed. You get your clothes on an' we'll go down t'

83rd an' catch the subway."

I didn't know about this: "Mom an' Dad'll see us."

"Naw they won't," said Crosley, rattling his whatchamacallits. "There's your gym shoes over in the corner there."

"One o' the laces is busted," I said.

"That's okay," said Crosley. "I'm here t' help ya, ain't I? Ain't I your Night Buddy?"

He shined the flashlight for me while I got dressed. Then it was shoelace time.

"Just sit on the bed an' stick your foot up here," he said, sliding his chair over. I sat down and stuck my foot out.

He took the busted shoelace in his big ol' claws and tried to tie it back together. He tried to tie it this way and that way, but whichever way he tried, the ends kept getting away from him. He even took the pieces out of the shoe and tried, but that didn't work either.

"BLORF!" he finally snorted, and reached down and got a fat rubber band off his bunch of whatchamacallits. He snapped it around my shoe, then hopped down on all four feet. "Okay, Big John, let's make tracks." He grinned up at me.

I still wasn't sure: "If ya really mean go out, we'll have t' pass right by the room where Mom an' Dad hang out."

"Not t' worry, ol' bud," said Crosley. "Ya see this right here?" He held out a flat glass thing on his bunch for me to look at. "I just hold this I-ain't-here doodad up an' nobody can see us. They can see everything *but* us. We'll just hafta be quiet, is all." He let the doodad go and put his flashlight in his pocket. That made it real dark.

"Come on now," said Crosley. "Hop on my back. An' keep your feet on top too. Come on —— "

I got off the bed and felt my way over. I bumped into him and climbed on and put my feet out in front.

"EXCELSIOR!" went Crosley *(too loud?)* and he reached up and pushed the bedroom door open! And then, real slow and quiet with me on top, he headed down the hall on his stumpy legs toward the stairs.

The front door was at the end of another hall downstairs, okay? But right next to this was the living room where Mom and Dad hung out. This was way cool, sure, but what if we got caught?

We started down the steps real careful. All the light there was was coming from the living room.

Crosley stuck the edge of the I-ain't-here doodad in his teeth when we got halfway down, then he kept on going. When we got to the bottom, there sat Mom and Dad, sure enough, right there in the living room. Dad was on the couch all into his tennis magazine, but Mom, hey! —— Mom had decided to look up right then and was looking right at where we were at! Oh man!

I grinned at her like an A-1 dork. I *felt* like an A-1 dork. But it was all totally weird. She kept looking and looking but she didn't grin back or get mad or anything. I waved just to make sure, but she still looked all blank. Crosley and me were headed straight for the front door with the I-ain't-here doodad winking in Crosley's teeth, and it was exactly like he had said: Mom looked and kept looking but she didn't see us at all!

We got to the door and watched Mom go back to her crossword puzzle. Then Crosley messed around with something on his belt and reached up and opened the door. Then he tiptoed outside with me on his back and clicked the door shut again!

CHAPTER TWO

Crosley and me were out there on the stoop watching the cars go by on West 87th Street. I got off his back and he stood up and we went down the steps to the sidewalk.

"Okay," he grinned, snapping the I-ain't-here doodad back with his other stuff. "We walk down t' 83rd an' catch the train, first thing. I'll tell ya all I know about it on the way."

I rubbed the seat of my pants: "Your hide sure is knotty, man. You'll tell me all ya know about what?"

Crosley looked sideways at me as we started off: "Why, all about the trouble over at the Pineapple Cheesecake Factory. Ya remember about that, don't ya, little buddy —— **YiGG,** I mean, ya remember about that, don't ya, John?"

"I'm not little!"

His eyes got big: "Jeeks, an' I should hope an' de*clare* ya ain't! An' anybody says different better look out, right?"

"*Right!* But listen, I better tell ya somethin', Crosley. I don't have a middle name. My name's just John Degraffenreidt."

"Hey, I *know.* That's one reason I picked ya for a Night Buddy. On account of I ain't got a middle name neither!"

We kept on walking.

"But most *people* do. An' that's what I am, ya know."

"Right," said Crosley. "That's right. But most people need three names just t' tell theirselves apart. You don't, awright, an' I'll tell ya why. If everybody else has a middle name *but* you, that makes ya special just by its own self, see? Ya don't even need t' be a crocodile or nothin'."

We turned the corner and started down the Avenue: "Hey," I grinned, "I guess I *don't, do* I?"

"Don't what, buddy?"

"Don't need t' be a crocodile."

"Nope."

There weren't a lot of people out on the sidewalks this late and Crosley walked fast.

"I'll start at the beginnin'," he said. "I'm at home asleep early yesterday, right? An' the phone rings. It's my brother Crenwinkle. He's the one keeps track of all this stuff. He says this manager over at the Pineapple Cheesecake Factory called him —— " Crosley pointed: "Remind me t' stop at that all-night drugstore up there, will ya, buddy?"

"Sure, Cros."

"Good deal. Anyhow, everything seems normal over at the Pineapple Cheesecake Factory, this manager tells Crenwinkle. Pineapple cheesecakes are scootin' right off the assembly line —— "

(Crosley pulled out a big red handkerchief and wiped the drool off his mouth.)

" —— an' goin' right into the boxes t' be shipped out. Everything looks normal, anyhow, till this truck driver comes back an' tells the manager the boxes he's picked up are empty! Boxes the manager's seen filled up with pineapple cheesecakes not ten minutes before that! *Jeeks*, John, I *ask* ya!"

"That's *crazy*," I said.

"An' ever since, the boxes have emptied out as quick as they get filled up," said Crosley. "An' the manager can't figure out how it's happenin'."

"That's simple," I said, jumping over a crack in the sidewalk. "Somebody's stealin' the pineapple cheesecakes."

"That's what *I* thought," said Crosley. "Only nobody else goes *in* there. It's all one big *machine,* an' all the manager does is turn it on an' off. He's been stayin' there all day an' all night watchin' everything. He finally called up Crenwinkle —— "

Just then this tiny little Chihuahua dog saw us coming from a long way away, and when we got up close, he decided Crosley needed to be destroyed. He yipped and snapped at him and snarled and jerked on his sparkly pink leash.

Crosley stood up on his back legs and unsnapped the I-ain't-here doodad and held it out: **"Yerk! Yerk! Yerk!** Step right up, Arnold, red crocodile rump roast! Come on an' take a bite!"

The little dog froze right in the middle of a yip. He stood there all bugeyed on his back legs and twisted back and forth.

"Yerk! Yerk! Yerk! Yerk!"

I kept on going down the street and the laugh followed along beside me.

"Yi!" went the little dog. *"Yik!"* And he started dancing around in circles and getting tangled up in his leash.

Crosley snapped the doodad back on his bunch and was right there with me again, grinning and bobbing along on his back legs. I tried to pretend like nothing happened.

"Here's the drugstore," I pointed.

"Oh yeah, thanks, buddyroo."

We went in the store and Cros got two real strong flashlight batteries, and on the way back out he picked up a pair of orange shoelaces.

The woman behind the cash register had on bright purple lipstick. "That'll be four-forty-eight," she said, squinting at her fingernails.

Crosley snapped a little card whatchamacallit off his belt with his picture on it. He held it up: "It's okay, this here's my I-D gimcrack."

The woman squinted at the gimcrack and popped her gum: "Why sure enough, Cros! An' hey, you an' John have yourselves a real excitin' Program, ya hear?"

NIGHT BUDDIES   AMALGAMATED

I-D GIMCRACK

Please give this crocodile anything
he needs without charge if you can.

He and John are out on an
Official Night Buddies Program.

WE HELP OUT

WE HELP OUT

NIGHT BUDDIES   AMALGAMATED

"You have a great night yourself," grinned Crosley, snapping the gimcrack back and putting the other stuff in his pockets.

"That's right," I said. "You have a great night, ma'am."

We started down the street again.

"So," Crosley said, "the manager finally phoned Crenwinkle."

"You didn't give the woman any money."

Crosley looked at me: "Ya didn't see her complain, did ya?"

"Nope."

"That's cause us Night Buddies get everything free when we're on a Program, awright? —— But the manager told Crenwinkle all about the mystery, see? An' Crenwinkle called me an' I said sure I'd take the assignment, had my new Night Buddy lined up too an' —— "

"Is Crenwinkle red like you, Cros?"

"Naw, buddy, he's just your regular green. I'm the only red one —— Anyhow, I said to 'im, sure, I'd handle it. It's pineapple cheesecakes we're talkin' about, after all." He grinned: "Ain't that right, ol' man?"

"It sure is," I said. "But ya know what, you're really not supposed t' say 'ain't.'"

"Har?" blinked Crosley. "Who says?"

"My mom an' dad. An' a whole lotta other people too."

"Well, ya know somethin'," said Crosley, "they're right." He walked along and scratched his head: "They're exackly right. That's just the way kids an' grownups are supposed t' talk. But ya see, with us crocodiles it's a little different situation. We got some special words that we have t' use just because we're crocodiles. We call 'em crocodile words an' we —— "

I cut in: "Is 'ain't' a crocodile word?"

"Yeah, that's one," said Crosley. "That's one o' the main ones."

"Hang on," I said. "Here's the stairs to the subway."

"Oh yeah, right."

When we got down to the bottom, nobody was there but a squatty little man asleep in the token booth. He had a big dead cigar in his mouth.

Crosley winked at me and tiptoed up to the window hole: ***"SCUSE ME!"***

The squatty little man's eyes jumped wide open and he chomped down on his cigar and looked around everywhere: ***"Hey! Who's got the chain saw! No chain saws allowed down here!"***

He looked real hard at me and Crosley: "You guys ain't runnin' a chain saw, are ya? That's positively against the rules!"

Crosley just grinned at him: "A subway token for my buddy an' one for me too, if ya please."

The squatty little man brightened right up: *"Sheesh,"* he said to Crosley. "That wuz *you?* I thought somebody'd brought a chain saw down here. Two tokens, that what ya said? That'll be five-even."

Crosley showed him the I-D gimcrack: "It's okay, Amalgamated Order o' Night Buddies."

The little man squinted at the gimcrack: "Oh, well, why *sure,"* he said. "Why didn't ya *say* so? Go right *ahead*, Cros, be my *guest!"* And he pushed the tokens out underneath the glass. "You an' Big John have yerselves a swell Program." He saluted us with his big dead cigar.

We thanked him and pushed through the turnstiles and went over by the tracks and waited, and pretty soon a train with **NIGHT FOLKS LIMITED** on it came rattling up and stopped. The doors opened and we got on. There were two nurses down at the end of the car with **NIGHT SHIFT** on their caps.

"Hi Crosley!" they waved. *"Hi John!"*

"Hi there, ladies," waved Crosley. *"How's it goin'?"* (I waved too.)

"Great you've teamed up together," said the nurses.

"Thanks," said Crosley. *"Yeah, you got that one right."*

Cros and me sat down next to each other, and the doors slid shut. The train started off with a jerk and a moan and started clattering, and in no time we were in a dark tunnel and couldn't see out. There were lots of lights inside the car, though.

Crosley stuck his front feet out and looked at them: "This business about the red, I guess ya wanna hear about that, right?"

I grinned and twisted around: "Sure I do, cause I never been on a train with a red crocodile before."

"**YERK! YERK!** Yeah, an' I bet ya never been on a train with one that was allergic t' water neither."

"Probly not," I said. "What d'ya mean?"

"I mean *me*," grinned Crosley. "Naw, no kiddin', buddy, allergic is when somethin' that's supposed t' be okay for ya ain't okay —— an' it messes ya up or makes ya sick, right? Like it just so happens that if I get any water on me, somethin' goofy happens an' I start doin' the Black Bottom an' can't stop. You ever heard o' that ol' dance from a long time ago, the Black Bottom? Naw? Anyhow, I start doin' it, an' sometimes it takes all day an' all night before I can quit. One time —— **YERK!** —— one time it happened when I was at the Super Bowl game, the time that woman spilled that fancy bottled water on my tail. You mighta seen it on TV, did ya? —— the way I jumped up an' boogied right down across the field an' on out the other side, did ya see it?"

"That was *you?* Okay, so what happened?"

Crosley grinned and rattled his whatchamacallits. "Well, buddy, I just Black Bottomed through the parkin' lot an' on outta town till I was lost out in the boondocks someplace. —— **YERK! YERK!** Hadda wait an' catch the bus back."

I was trying to quit laughing: "Hey, that is just so *neat.* What's the Black Bottom look like?"

"Show ya later," said Crosley. "It's pretty fantastic. Not near enough space in here."

"Then tell me about the red."

"I'm *tellin'* ya," said Crosley. "That's *part* of it."

The train slowed down. We rumbled into a lighted station and stopped. The door opened and the nurses waved and got off, and then an all-night hamburger man in a red and yellow-striped hamburger suit got on.

"Hiya there, Cros!" he yelled. *"I see ya got John."*

"How's yourownself!" waved Crosley. *"Yeah, me an' Big John got us a job o' work tonight."*

The train started up again and Crosley smoothed out his yellow suit: "After that Super Bowl adventure, I called Crenwinkle. Crenwinkle's the big genius in the family, besides handlin' all the business calls that come in. I told 'im about water makin' me do the Black Bottom, told 'im it was gettin' t' be a nuisance —— "

"Hey, look," I pointed, "we're not underground anymore!"

Crosley turned and looked out at all the lighted

buildings flashing by.

"Sorry," I said. "Finish tellin' me about bein' red."

"Almost done, big guy. Like I said, I told Crenwinkle. About the Black Bottom an' all. An' he made me up these special pills t' take anytime I get water on me. They're what ya call antidotes. They stop the Black Bottom business in two minutes flat. The only thing is, I turn red from takin' 'em, okay? —— Not that I mind, understand? Not that I mind that part a *bit*. Cause when people see me now, they know not t' get me wet."

"I guess ya have t' carry the pills with ya all the time."

"Sure do," said Crosley, and he reached in his pocket and got me out this little bottle. Inside were lots and lots of tiny pills the size of BBs. Here's what it said on the label:

For My Brother Crosley
Take One of These Little Pills to
Stop Black Bottoming. If It's
Especially Bad, You May Take Two of
Them. And Try to Stay Dry.
    Fraternally,
    Crenwinkle

"They're black," I said, handing the bottle back.

Crosley stuck it in his pocket. "That's cause they're for the Black Bottom."

"Then how come they turn ya red?"

"You'll have t' ask Crenwinkle about that," said Crosley. "Somethin' about 'em gettin' tied up in my growlin' green gustibus juices. Somethin' along them lines, an' anyhow, Crenwinkle always colors his pills by what they stop, not by what they start."

"Say *what?*"

"They work good," winked Crosley. "But I still have t' be careful. Like I only take a bath in apple juice, things like that."

The train slowed down again. "The manager's meetin' us at this stop, buddy. We need t' get off."

CHAPTER THREE

The train stopped at the station and the door slid open. We waved goodbye to the all-night hamburger man and got off on the platform. We looked around but didn't see anybody anywhere.

"That's funny," said Crosley. "I wonder where the manager got to."

"Why don't you open your *eyes?*" said this squeaky voice from way up somewhere.

I saw where it came from first because I looked up first. I looked up and saw this big pineapple cheesecake beltbuckle. And then I looked up higher, and even higher than that, and finally all the way up at the round brown face of the biggest tallest woman in —— I don't know, the northern hemisphere or something. I mean at least. The pie-sized beltbuckle looked little on her, and the two big posts I thought held the roof up were the woman's giant legs!

"I'm Big Foot Mae," she yipped in that squeaky high voice. "I'm the manager." She had on coveralls the color of graham crackers, with pictures of pineapples all over them, and she had an oilcan in a holster too.

Crosley leaned back and grinned at her: "Top o' the evenin' to ya, Big Foot. I'm Crosley, an' this here's John."

"Brother Crenwinkle *said* you'd be bringin' your

new Night Buddy," she grinned back. "*Broke down, young guy, gimme some* low —— "

She reached her hand down and it was like slapping hands with a car seat. She had on this one glove that had just one finger to it, and I saw something else too before she straightened up.

"What's all those white specks in your hair?"

Her big hand felt up there: "Yeah, mm-hm, that's wood glue. Stuff keeps drippin' down on me inside the factory. Hey, come on along, though. Come on an' see for yourself. No good standin' round here!"

She took us out to the parking lot and we all climbed in her long graham cracker-colored van. There wasn't any front seat on Mae's side because Mae had to sit in the back seat just to get her legs in.

Crosley took the front seat on the other side, and I sat behind him and turned and checked out in back. And hey, the whole back part of the van, all the way to the back door, was heaped with thousands and thousands of little squiggly pieces of black wood. They were all kinds of shapes and had little white dots and smears on them.

Big Foot Mae saw me looking: "You got the roundest big ol' brown eyes. An' you wonderin' what that stuff is, right?" She started the engine and backed up.

"I *know* what it is. It's pieces to a puzzle."

The van stopped with a jerk: *"Well I just be dog! How'd you know?"*

"Cause," I said. "I seen pieces to a puzzle lot o' times, an' that's what those are. I never seen that many, though, an' no pictures on 'em."

"Well drop me down in the driveway if you ain't *sump'm!"* tweeted the giant woman. "Tellin' you *what!"* And she put the van in gear and started us off down the dark street to the Pineapple Cheesecake Factory.

"YERK! YERK! YERK! YERK!" chuckled Crosley.

Mae drove fast, and before anybody could think of anything else to say, we came to a long narrow building with a big pineapple cheesecake sign in front like this:

THE WORLD'S ONLY
PINEAPPLE CHEESECAKE FACTORY,
PERIOD

The building had a great big door at both ends for trucks to back up to, and there was one regular door in the middle. The only parking place had its own sign:

> ## NOBODY ELSE BETTER PARK HERE BUT BIG FOOT MAE.
> *(NOT THAT NOBODY NEEDS TO.)*

We all got out of the van, and Mae unlocked the middle door and let us inside the factory. She turned on the lights.

And that, let me tell you, was one far-out place. It was this one long, long room, and filling up most all of it was this huge orange machine that started at one end where the trucks came to put in the cream cheese and butter and sugar and stuff, and ended at the other end where it boxed up the finished pineapple cheesecakes for the other trucks to take away.

The walls and the floor were white, and the ceiling was white too, except for a large, crazy-shaped black part of it that went from above the middle door across to the machine, and then all the way over to the truck door at one end. There were little white dots and smears all over it.

Mae saw Crosley and me looking.

"Well now ya know. Now ya know what I do t' keep busy round here. Look there, you two, see them switches up on the wall yonder?"

She pointed at two big buttons way over the middle door. The brown one said *PINEAPPLE CHEESECAKES* underneath, and the black one said *NO PINEAPPLE CHEESECAKES.*

"Uh-huh," said Crosley. "Yeah, I see 'em. What about it?"

"What's wrong wid you?" squeaked the giant woman. "They're why I'm *manager* here, an' why I got this button-pushin' glove on. I'm the only one can reach that high, man. They're why I got my Ceilin' t' keep me occupied too."

"Har?" said Crosley, scratching his head.

"No lie," said Mae. "Just pushin' a button when it's time t' start Jones an' another one when it's time t' stop Jones —— "

"Wait a second," I said. "Who's Jones?"

"He's the machine," said Mae. "Anyhow, that's all I'm give t' *do* round here, push them two buttons.

I'm tellin' you I'd get mighty low if I didn't have my Project t' keep busy on."

"So you're doin' a puzzle," I said, looking up.

"Sure am," yipped Mae. "But hey, big guy, this ain't no regular puzzle. Somethin' simple like that wouldn't last. Naw," she said, waving a big arm at the Ceiling: "This is what you call your Grand Project. This, brothers, ain't just a True Puzzle of All the Stars in the Sky at Night, but of All the New Ones They Keep Comin' Up With!"

"Well," I said, "I guess that explains why you're puttin' it on the ceiling."

The big woman nodded: "Right one more time. I'm able t' reach up there, first off. An' second off, how you guess it would look t' have the sky down in the floor? Hm? I'm waitin' for an answer."

I pointed at her: "I bet that's why ya got glue in your hair too."

"John, you about t' wear me out." Mae grinned at Crosley: "Your new Night Buddy's sharp. Just like Brother Crenwinkle said."

Crosley was squinting up at the stars in the Ceiling. "That's right, Mae, Big John ain't got no middle name neither —— But looka here, what in the world do ya call that squiggly-lookin' bunch o' stars up over the door there —— ?"

"Them? Oh, right, that's the Corkscrew Constellation Right Yonder." Mae got some new pieces out of her pocket and studied them. "Yeah, an' now that you bring it up, I bet these very pieces'll fit right in beside 'em!"

She rumbled over to the door and got a little squirt bottle of glue out of another pocket and squirted glue on the backs of the new pieces. And then, not even needing to stretch, she reached up and stuck them right next to the Corkscrew Constellation Right Yonder on the Ceiling.

"They *do* fit there! I *knew* it! Thank you so much, Brother Crosley!"

"Don't give it a thought. Hey, lissen, ya got some more glue in your hair in back —— "

"Hey, listen you two —— "

Crosley and Mae turned around and looked at me. I tried to look serious.

"I thought we came here about the pineapple cheesecake trouble."

Crosley and Mae grinned at each other.

"An' here I stand mutterin' on my two back feet,"

said Crosley. "Me that's been worried half in two about the pineapple cheesecakes. Say, Mae, did ya know I'm King o' the Hogs about pineapple cheesecakes?"

Mae made a sick face: "Naw, I didn't. Can't abide the things myself. Been around too many *of* 'em. But I do so love workin' on my Puzzle! Mm-hm, an' all this trouble has been gettin' in the way."

"I ate sixty-seven of 'em one time," said Crosley. "An' still couldn't stop. Ya see this tooth missin' here —— ?"

He held the side of his mouth open.

" —— Crenwinkle had t' pull it out an' run a tube through an' wire my mouth shut. An' then he pumped me with Campbell's Clam Bisque through the tube till the cravin' let up."

Brown Mae had turned kind of gray.

"Hey, I ain't makin' ya sick, am I?" said Crosley. "Ya look a little delicate."

"Crosley, come on, how about it!" I said.

"Har? —— What did ya —— Oh yeah, right! Hey, lissen, Big Foot, where izzit ya said all the trouble was? Let's get t' work, awright? Ain't it high time we got started?"

"It's been high time," sighed Mae. "But ya see,

that's part of the trouble: I don't know where the trouble is *at*. It's like I tole Professor Crenwinkle —— everything works fine till the pineapple cheesecakes get boxed up, an' then the truck drivers come t' get 'em an' all of a sudden they're gone. There's just boxes with nothin' inside! Hey, if I knew where the problem started, I'd not be interviewin' *you*."

"Turn Jones on an' lemme look," said Crosley.

Mae rumbled over and reached way up and pushed the brown *PINEAPPLE CHEESECAKES* button.

A sweet humming noise started. It sounded like a church organ stuck on one soft note.

The belt on the machine started moving, and down at one end the cream cheese and eggs and sugar and other stuff popped up on it and rode along till it all went in a big mixer.

Then, after everything got mixed up, it got poured in aluminum pie pans with graham cracker crusts that ran by underneath.

Crosley followed along watching real hard.

After the pouring part came the cooking. The filled-up pans rode the belt inside a little oven-house, and the house door closed and an orange light blinked on for a minute. Then it blinked off and another door opened on the other side, and the pans came out on the belt all steamy.

Crosley watched, and his eyes were getting bigger and rounder.

"Ut! Ut!" I shouted, **"Crosley, you're droolin' all on the floor!"**

"Yigg!" yelped Crosley. He yanked out a big red handkerchief and wiped his big red mouth. "Mighty sorry about that, folks. It just smelled so super incredible."

"Don't worry yourself," said Mae. "Over here now is where the cheesecakes get t' be *pineapple* cheesecakes —— "

We went over to where four pipes hung down right over the belt. The regular old cheesecakes ran by underneath, and the first pipe, the biggest, dropped crushed pineapple on top of each one. Then the other pipes dropped cornstarch, sugar, and a squirt of lemon juice. Finally the cheesecakes rode into another oven-house and got cooked some more.

When they came out, they were *pineapple* cheesecakes!

"Excelsior!" hollered Crosley, watching them ride by under his nose. He was drooling again, but I decided I might just as well let him.

And then **CLACK!** Crosley snapped his mouth shut and shoved himself away from Jones. "Yeah, awright —— Awright, so why don't ya show me the rest o' the operation, Mae."

"Come on," squeaked Mae. "Right on over here. See the pineapple cheesecakes gettin' shut up in boxes, right there after the tops go on? An' see there how the belt keeps goin' an' sets the boxes down for the trucks t' pick up?"

"Yeah, I see it," said Crosley. "You see it there, John?"

"Yop."

Mae pointed to the boxes piling up by the truck door. "Go on," she waved her huge hand. "Go on over an' open one up an' help yourself, Brother Crosley."

Crosley drooled heavy: "Ya *mean* that? Hey, ya *mean* it? Awright, Big Foot, if ya say so, I don't mind if I do —— "

And he went right over to the last box that had been filled up and tore it open. He stared inside, then turned as pink as cotton candy and fell back into Mae's knees and tripped her. They both fell on the floor, and when Mae landed, the building bounced and several hundred puzzle pieces rattled down off the Ceiling.

"GREAT GRANDADDY CRANWELL'S PET CRAWFISH!" Crosley roared, and it sounded like eight chain saws going at once. *"THE FOOL BOX IS EMPTY! THERE AIN'T A PINEAPPLE CHEESECAKE IN THERE NOPLACE!"*

CHAPTER FOUR

I ran over to the pineapple cheesecake box and looked inside: *"Ut!* You're right, Crosley, there's nothin' in here."

"Just like I tole you," squeaked Mae. She was still down there on the floor next to Crosley. "Just like I tole Brother Crenwinkle."

"But I just seen 'em go in the *box,*" wailed Crosley.

"That's right," I said. "I saw 'em go in too."

"So now I guess you got some notion o' what's been happenin'," Mae answered. "What I want t' know is, can you help out? I can't work on my Puzzle with all this devilin' me."

And she got up and banged around slow, picking up the pieces that had come down off the Ceiling.

Crosley laid all the way down on his back right now and started to think. He thought for a pretty long time, and while he thought his red color came back.

"Hey!" he jumped up and yelled, *"Lissen, I got an idea ——— "*

Mae and me stood there looking at him.

"Lissen," said Crosley. "Here's what we do. Mae, you go over an' cut Jones off ——— "

Mae thudded over like he said to and reached up pushed the black button.

The sweet humming stopped and so did the belt.

Crosley scooted down to the boxing up place and looked in an open box and made sure it was full of pineapple cheesecakes.

CLACK! "——Hey, lissen," he said, "I promise not t' drool on 'em."

He went over to where the boxes got closed up. He opened one and *it* was full of pineapple cheesecakes. And so was the next one and the next one.

But when he opened the box right after that, he jumped back ——— *"John! Hey Big Foot! Come here an' lookit!"*

We ran over and looked inside the box, and it

was empty! Not only empty, but the bottom of it was ripped open, and a big square pipe two times as wide as Crosley was attached to it and went down through a hole in the floor!

"Awright," said Crosley. "Yeah, Mae, now I think we're gettin' someplace. Go turn Jones back on, quick —— "

The giant woman went over and pushed the brown button and the machine started humming again.

"Lookit underneath here," Crosley pointed. "Just past the pipe. Ya see that contraption closin' the box bottoms back up again?"

"We sure do." (Mae and me said it together.)

Then we opened the rest of the boxes all the way to the pickup door and they were empty too.

"Big Foot," Crosley said, turning to her and holding his front legs out sideways: "Big Foot, I got a flash for ya."

"A flash? What ya mean flash?"

"Big Foot," Crosley said, "it's Jones that's been purloinin' your pineapple cheesecakes."

Mae staggered backward: *"Naw!* How can *that* be? Jones don't eat pineapple cheesecakes. Jones don't even *like* pineapple cheesecakes. *I* sure don't."

"That ain't what I said," blinked Crosley. "I said the thing's been rippin' 'em *off*. Somebody's rigged it so it pulls 'em outta the boxes an' dumps 'em down that hole in the floor there."

"Oh my stars an' sweatsocks!" said Mae.

"Oh mine too," said Crosley. "Yeah, an' where the things end up after that's anybody's guess. Ain't that so, John? *Hey, where are ya?*"

"It sure is so," I hollered back. I was crawling around under the machine looking.

"Hey, ya know, Crosley, we really oughta pull this pipe away an' look an' see where this hole goes to."

Crosley and Mae grinned at each other like before.

"YERK! YERK! Okay, John, let's do it! Let's pull the pipe away! You grab that side, an' I'll reach around you an' —— *PULL NOW!"*

We pulled, and then we stopped and pulled harder, and all of a sudden the big pipe broke away from the floor and we fell back with it right into Mae.

She rubbed her leg: "Man, Crosley, you knotty as a waffle iron."

"Whad ya expect? Smooth as a baby's bottom?"

"Hey," I said, "come on, let's see where the hole goes to."

Crosley straightened out his yellow suit, and Mae straightened her big belt buckle, and we all crowded under Jones and looked down the hole.

Something stunk.

"Smells like lizards," said Mae. "I can't see nothin', though."

Crosley shined his flashlight down inside.

"Hey look," I pointed. "It's green. I mean the sides are green, kinda like Mom's yukky baked spinach."

"An' square too," said Mae. "With them little pipes runnin' all down one side." She reached her big arm in: "Slippery too!"

"Slippery, ya say? Hmmm ——— " Crosley laid

back down in his thinking position with his eyes shut and his front feet behind his head, and while he did, Mae and me got the flashlight and looked inside the hole again. It went down and down on a slant and never seemed to stop.

"What's lizards smell like?" I asked her.

"Like this: Here, smell my hand ——— "

"EXCELSiOR!" roared Crosley, jumping up right **NOW** and **"YiGG!"** ——— smacking his head under the machine.

"What happened?" we yelled.

Crosley rubbed the top of his head and grinned big: "Lissen, you citizens, I *got* it! It just come t' me what's been happenin' here!"

"*What?*" Mae squealed. "*Tell* us!"

Crosley pointed to the hole: "It all come t' me when ya said about the smell again ——— "

"Ya mean like lizards?" I said.

"Right, an' about the green an' slippery."

He stopped now and grinned at us so big and bright we had to shade our eyes.

"Well *tell* us!" yipped Mae.

"Okay, I'll tell ya. Awright. The first thing is, the hole's square so the pineapple cheesecakes won't flip over while they're slidin' down."

"*I* got *that* much figured out," said Mae.

"An' it's slippery so they'll slide good," said Crosley.

"Might just as well go on an' tell us why it's green," Mae fussed. "Long as you won't get t' the point!"

"I was workin' up t' that," snorted Crosley. "As I was *tryin'* t' say, I started thinkin' pineapple cheese-cakes, an' about slippery stuff an' all, an' then when ya started in again about the lizard smell, it come t' me ———"

"Ya mean it *came* to ya," I said. "*Come's* not a crocodile word. Is it?"

"Awright," said Mae. "What *came* to ya? What?"

Crosley grinned and got up: "*Holy Begonias,* I said t' myself. This, I said, has gotta be the work o' the Iguana Gang! Those pirates are back in business again!"

"What in the name o' nastiness is the Iguana Gang?" said Mae.

"What's *Iguanas?*" I said.

"Iguanas," explained Crosley, "are big ol' slippery lizards. At least this gang's slippery. An' they're robbers too. That's what they do all the time. Steal stuff. Oh yeah, an' lissen, Big Foot ———"

"I'm listenin'."

"The hole's green cause iguanas are green, yellow, an' black, okay? I mean, since ya asked me ———"

"Say *what?*" blinked Mae.

"Iguanas," waved Crosley, "are green, yellow, and black. But green's their favorite color."

"Okay. I got that. But please tell me just one more thing ———"

Cros sniffed: "Ask right on."

"Tell me what them little pipes goin' down that one side's for."

Crosley thought a couple seconds: "I dunno. Can you dope it out, John?"

I tugged on a curl: "Nope, I got no clue what they are."

Crosley thought a little more, then reached down and snapped a ball whatchamacallit off his belt: "Here, Mae. Okay, what I want ya t' do, I want ya t' stay right here next t' the hole an' hang onto this here gizmo. Ya see how rope comes out of it kinda gradual if ya pull?"

Mae pulled some out: "Mm-hm, yeah."

"Crenwinkle made it. It's got three miles o' rope inside, an' I'm thinkin' me an' my buddy here'll just hang onto one end an' let ourselves down the hole an' see if we can't get all this purloinin' put t' rest. What d'ya say, John, ya ain't scared, are ya?"

"Uh —— Nope, not me."

"Ya sure?"

"Sure I'm sure."

"Great," said Crosley, "cause it's a true fact that I sure ain't. Awright, Mae, you hang onto the rope gizmo real good an' we'll see ya the next time we see ya!"

Then he backed into the hole real slow with the rope gizmo in his teeth: "Okay, John, get on my shoulders now an' sit tight."

I got on and he waved: "Areeva-durchie, Big Foot!"

"What you gonna *do?*" said the worried face up there above us.

"Beats me," winked Crosley. "Lissen out down the hole, though. Maybe ya'll hear somethin'."

"Hold on just a second," said Mae.

"What izzit now?" said Crosley.

"How come you red?" said Mae.

Crosley held up the bottle of little pills for her to look at.

"Oh, right, I see," said Mae. "They get all tied up in your growlin' green gustibus juices."

"Bingo," said Crosley. And as soon as he said it,

he stuffed the pills back in his pocket and let loose with his feet, and him and me started sliding down the spooky green hole into the dark.

CHAPTER FIVE

"So how ya doin' up there, buddy?" said the chain saw. It was really Crosley, right? Him and me had slid a long way down the tunnel already and we couldn't see a thing. There was just the spooky dark and the lizard smell.

"I'm okay," I said. "Except your knotty shoulders are pokin' me."

"Jeeks, shoulda remembered! Here, sit on this ____"

"What is it?" I said. It felt soft.

"Your standard frammis for sittin' on crocodiles. It blows up into a cushion soon as I snap it offa my belt."

"Thanks. Hey, yeah, I can't feel your hickeys now."

"I can't feel your sitdown neither. ***YERK! YERK! YERK!***"

It was black dark and we slid down and down on the end of the Crenwinkle rope.

But just then Crosley reached his claws out and stopped us ——

"What?" I said.

"Felt somethin' with my tail. Lessee —— Yeah. There's a hole on the side just underneath here ——"

He let us down a little more, and then, right there next to us, was another tunnel going straight off to the side. Crosley clicked on the flashlight.

This new tunnel was slippery and green like the one we were already in. But it smelled kinda sweet for a change, and it went sideways instead of down, and right where it started was this sign:

**TO FORBIDDEN
STORAGE BIN
NUMBER ONE
→**

"What d'ya think, Big John? Ya figure we oughta check it out?"

"Don't ya guess we better?"

"Well, I guess so," gulped Crosley. "Okay, slide the frammis down my back an' lay on it with the flashlight. Here we go —— "

"Right —— "

We left the Crenwinkle rope hanging there and started into the side tunnel.

It was all level now, and we had the flashlight and could see the creepy green walls close around us and all dark up ahead. Crosley crawled along for several minutes and it started getting chillier and chillier. And then we crawled around a sharp turn in the tunnel and right out into this huge cold cave with this big green lamp hanging down in the middle on a cord. And piled up high around the lamp, from the floor to the ceiling and from one wall to the other, were sixty-seven thousand, one hundred and eighty-nine pineapple cheesecakes! (That's what it said on the sign hanging on the lamp.)

"Holy hubcaps an' ham biscuits!" said Crosley. I got off him and we stood up in the middle of it all. "We sure found out where they all got to, didn't we, buddy?"

I shivered in my t-shirt and stared at the monster stacks of pineapple cheesecakes. "Yeah, Crosley, we sure did. They look kinda yukky in this green light, though, don't they?"

"——Whad ya say? Sorry, buddy, I wasn't payin' attention."

"Ut! Ut! Crosley, you're droolin' all on the floor again!"

Crosley didn't hear me this time either. He was staring around at all those stacks, and his eyes were getting wider and rounder.

Dribble! Slobber!

"HEY CROSLEY!"

" —— Har?"

I gave him a real hard look.

"Come on, Crosley, what're we gonna do? You're not gonna stand here all night droolin', are ya?"

CLACK! went Crosley's jaws, and he shut his eyes real tight. He pulled out his big red handkerchief and wiped his mouth. It took a minute before he opened his eyes.

"Awright," he blinked. "I'm awright now. Thanks for rescuin' me. I almost tore into one o' them stacks for half a second there."

"We better go," I shivered.

"Yeah."

So I climbed back on him and we started back out through the side tunnel.

When we got to the main tunnel, Crosley chomped down on the Crenwinkle rope, and I got up on his shoulders, and we started down again. But we slid only a little way before Crosley stopped and said he felt another side tunnel.

We turned on the flashlight and started in, and there, just like last time, was a forbidden sign, but this time with a number two on it. And at the other end of the tunnel, just like before, was another cold green cave full of pineapple cheesecakes. This one had seventy-three thousand, four hundred and four.

I pulled on Crosley's yellow sleeve: "Come on, let's go —— "

"Awww —— " But he made himself turn away and I rode him back out to the main tunnel.

We grabbed the rope and slid down some more.

And we found another side tunnel with another cave full of pineapple cheesecakes. And right after that we found another one. And then another one. Until finally we had discovered seventeen caves, each one cold and spooky, with a green lamp hanging down in the middle of piles and piles and piles of pineapple cheesecakes.

Crosley and me were standing there in the seventeenth one, scoping out exactly fifty-one thousand and eight of the things.

"I ain't believin' this," mumbled Crosley. "I just ain't believin' this." His eyes were all glassy, and he was turning pink. "This here really is too much. An' t' think I ain't even ate one!" He wiped his dripping mouth with his dripping handkerchief.

"That was tough, Cros, wasn't it?"

We were back out at the main tunnel.

"Yeah," sighed Crosley. "That was a mean one."

"Crosley —— ?"

"Mm?"

"I'm proud of you, Crosley, okay?"

"Well thanks, ol' buddy. I'm real glad."

"Anyway, I hope there aren't any more pineapple cheesecakes. I'm gettin' awful tired o' lookin' at 'em."

"Well, I guess there's just one way t' find out," said Crosley. "Ya ain't gettin' scared or nothin'?"

"Who —— me?"

"Okay, then." **CLACK!** "Here we go —— "

We started back down, and this time we slid a long way and didn't see any more side tunnels.

"Gosh," I said, "what if it just never stops goin' down? What about that, Crosley?"

Crosley started to answer but he never got to. Because just then the rope popped loose up above us, and before Crosley could reach out and stop us, we were shooting down through the dark like a roller-coaster at the park.

"I'M KINDA SCARED NOW!" I hollered.

"YIGG! WHAT HAPPENED?" yelled Crosley. **"OH YIGG! HEY, NOTHIN' T' WORRY ABOUT!"**

We fell and fell. And there wasn't anything we could do to stop so we kept right on falling.

And then we flew past an electric sign on the wall. There wasn't time to read it; we just saw the arrow on it pointing down.

By this time we were starting to think we really *might* fall down the hole forever, so we did the only thing we could: we shut our eyes and hoped not.

And almost as soon as we did, no kidding, the tunnel started leveling out! It slanted down a little bit less and a little bit less, till finally it didn't slant at all. And that's right where it ended and Crosley and me popped out of it like two corks —— right into another great big cave.

We slid to a stop and jumped up and looked around. There weren't any pineapple cheesecakes for sure, not anywhere. But there was a yellow picnic table with six chairs. And three double-decker beds with black blankets. And a green floor and ceiling and walls with lots of black and yellow blotches. And a giant chandelier with hundreds of twinkling green bulbs and pieces of glass hanging down on a black chain.

And a strong smell of **SOMETHING** was

coming out of a room on the other side of the cave.

Crosley looked back at the tunnel and growled: "Fine thing! Ya heard me tell Mae t' hang onto the rope gizmo, right?"

I started to say yes. But just then a whole mile of rope came flapping and flopping out of the tunnel and dumped down all over Crosley. And then **Boκ!** The gizmo on the other end flew out and hit him right on the side of the head!

"Ha! Ha! Ha! Ha!" I giggled. *"Hee! Hee! Hee!* Oh hey, I hope it didn't hurt your head, Crosley. It didn't, did it?"

Crosley just sat there under the rope looking steamed.

"Here," I said. "Lemme help get that off ya ——"

"Leave the big salamander under it!" hissed voices. **"He's rat where he oughta be!"**

"WHO'S CALLIN' ME A SALAMANDER!" roared Crosley, fighting out from under the rope.

"WHO SAID THAT? I BET I KNOW WHO SAID IT!"

"If yew'd read the signs lak yore supposed to, yew wootn't need t' ask," snarled the voices.

CHAPTER SIX

Crosley and me looked toward the room with the **SMELL** where the snarly voices came from, and there stood four ugly iguanas in green gym shorts, squirting their long tongues in and out of their faces. There were two pairs of them, really, because half had on yellow undershirts and half had on black ones.

"Whut's the matter, salamander?" smirked the yellow undershirts. "Ain't yew growed-up enough t' read? Rat there's a sign just lak the one yew slid past." They pointed to this one by the tunnel:

PRIVATE UNDERGROUND
HANGOUT AND KITCHEN
OF THE THIEVING
IGUANA GANG

And then this one:

> ## No Crocodiles Allowed!
> ## Speshly Crawzly!

The strange little pipes ran out of the tunnel too, right past the signs, and went back and forth across the ceiling.

Crosley looked around the place: "I don't care about your dumb signs. We woulda come anyhow, ya slimy crooks."

"Lissen at the big salamander," hissed the black undershirts. "An' whut yew figger on doin' while yore here, salamander?"

"Whut's all thet racket?" snarled still more voices. Then two new iguanas with green shorts and no shirts swaggered in from the stinky room.

"It's Crawzly," snarled the yellows. "An' he's got thet twine-headed brat John Grassinreeds wid 'im."

"Him wid them big ol' round eyes?"

"Thet's him."

"They ditn't see the sign up the Loot Chute?" hissed no shirts.

"Says they'd o' come anyhow," snarled the blacks,

shooting their tongues in and out.

I walked right up to the new iguanas so they wouldn't think I was scared: "Hey, how come you two don't have any shirts on?"

"It's our night t' cook, boy," they hissed. "Gits hot in there. Anyhow, whut's thet dumb rubber band doin' on yore dumb tennis shoe?"

Crosley came over next to me: "They cook all the time, ol' buddy. When they ain't eatin' their swill or else out robbin' somebody." (He pointed to the stinky room.) "They mix jellybeans an' lizard cheese up in a puddin' in there an' don't eat nothin' else! Every day an' every night it's jellybeans an' lizard cheese, lizard cheese an' jellybeans! That's that smell ya smell now."

"YUKK!" I said and held my nose.

"They never smile neither," said Crosley, "cause it sticks in their teeth so bad."

The yellows smirked: "Yore a fine one t' talk about *our* food."

"Yeah," hissed the blacks. "Anybody thet eats pineapple cheesecakes oughta keep his rusty ol' trap shut."

Crosley's jaw dropped wide open! "What in the world're ya talkin' about? What's the matter with pineapple cheesecakes? Just tell me that! An' anyhow,

I eat other stuff. Campbell's Clam Bisque an' —— "

"Eatin' just one bite would make us sick till two weeks after Christmas," groaned the skins. ***"SOO-WEE!"***

Crosley pointed at the kitchen: "You musta heaved up all over Santa Claus from eatin' *that* stuff!"

The yellows spat their tongues in and out: "Anybody thet eats pineapple cheesecakes must have pineapple cheesecakes for armpits," they hissed. "Just thankin' about it's makin' as dizzy." And they shut their eyes and rolled their heads all around.

I took a deep breath: "If you guys hate pineapple cheesecakes so bad, then how come ya been stealin' all of 'em?"

"How come yew ain't got no middle name?" smirked both blacks.

"I'll tell ya why they do it," said Crosley. "It's the way these lizards operate. They pick out somethin' a whole lotta people like, an' then they go out an' steal it all up an' hold it for ransom."

"Ya mean like —— "

"You know, when ya make somebody pay t' get their own stuff back," said Crosley, looking hard at the Iguana Gang.

"Thassrat, yew big salamander," they all snarled together. "We're gonna tell Big Butt Mae about it in the mornin' an' whut're yew fixin' t' do about thet?"

"Ya can bet we'll do *somethin'*," snorted Crosley. "Ain't that right, Big John?"

"That's right!" I said.

"Hig! Hig! Hig! Hig!" cackled the Iguana Gang. And they cackled so hard the giant chandelier tinkled on its chain. *"Hig! Hig! Hig! Hig! Hig!"*

"I don't guess it'd do any good," sighed Crosley, "t' ask ya t' be nice an' take the pineapple cheesecakes back where ya got 'em from?"

"Aw, Hig! Hig! Hig! Hig! Hig!" squealed the iguanas, and they grabbed their bellies and held on. *"Hig! Hig! Hig! Aw, Hig! Hig! Hig!"*

"Naw," muttered Crosley. "I didn't figure it'd do any good."

And he lay right down there in the middle of the floor and shut his eyes and locked his front feet behind his head.

"Hey salamander!" squawked the blacks, *"this ain't no flophouse. Whut yew thank yore doin'?"*

"I *know* what I'm doin'," said Crosley. "I'm thinkin'. Shuddup."

And he lay there and thought. And nothing came to him so he squinched his eyes tighter and thought harder and it was right then that I scooted over and whispered.

"Hey Crosley —— "

Crosley's eyes popped open: "Fup! —— *Har?"*

"Excelsior, Crosley!"

"What, buddy? Ya mean ya got a plan?"

"I'm not sure," I whispered. *"Listen, first off, we gotta sneak outta here like we did at my place, okay?"*

"Right with ya so far, chief."

☆ ☆ ☆

"Whut yew doin', squirt?" the skins hollered. *"Hey, look, little big-eyes is fixin' t' ride the salamander! Hey, squirt —— **Hig! Hig!** —— don't hang yore feet over or yew'll git floor burns! **Hig! Hig! Hig!"***

Then the whole gang started squealing and cackling again, and they did it so hard they forgot to watch. And when they stopped and looked around again, Crosley and me had vanished!

"Thet's cockeyed," snarled the yellows. *"Hey, salamander, where yew at?"*

We didn't make a sound, and the iguanas started searching all over everywhere.

"*Hey, squirt,*" squawked the blacks, "*we ain't playin' hide-n-seek. Show yore stupid self!*"

We didn't make a peep. Then the yellows and blacks looked under the double-decker beds, and the skins ran in the kitchen and looked everywhere —— inside the lizard cheese closet and even in the big jellybean pot —— but nobody could find me and Crosley.

"**SHEESH!**" they all hissed. "Them two's hidin' someplace in our own hideout, an' we don't lak it a-tall!"

We had got out the I-ain't-here doodad is what it was. And as soon as we were invisible, we had snuck in the kitchen and were sitting in there waiting.

"*Those slimebags called me little,*" I whispered.

"*Button up,*" Crosley whispered back. "*Yeah, I heard 'em. Just keep still an' tell me the plan.*"

"*Okay,*" I whispered. "*But there's one thing I can't figure out.*"

"*Run it by me,*" Crosley whispered back. "*Ain't I your Night Buddy?*"

"*I sure hope so,*" I whispered. "*Okay, first of all —— *"

The iguanas tore all over the place searching. The yellows looked under the table and chairs, and one yellow even climbed up and looked in the giant chandelier while a black held a ladder for him. The skins checked the kitchen again, then ran up the tunnel to search.

Crosley whispered, *"Okay, I think I got that base covered."*

"How ya gonna do it?" I whispered back.

"Show ya on the way," whispered Crosley. *"Come on, we better hurry."*

Then I rode him tiptoeing over to the lizard cheese closet, and we carried the stuff, hunk by stinking hunk, across to the fireplace and stuffed it up the chimney.

"Yigg!" croaked Crosley, who had to carry it in his mouth. *"Uk! Oh, Yigg!"*

"Button up now," I whispered back, but I was making an invisible sick face myself.

When we had jammed all the lizard cheese up the chimney, we dragged the big jellybean pot over and stuffed it up too. Then we sat down against the wall to wait some more.

Pretty soon the skins slid down out of the tunnel looking mighty mad.

"They ain't up the Loot Chute," they snarled to the yellows and blacks.

Then they all looked steamed, and they plopped down at the table and shot their tongues in and out.

"Ya got the doodad?" whispered Crosley.

"Yeah," I whispered back.

"Awright, hang on ——— "

And we started off as soft as we could out of the kitchen into where the iguanas were!

"Stupid salamander!" growled one of the blacks. "He's crazy if he thanks he can fool us, ain't he?"

The others around the table hissed and flicked out their tongues.

And right then Crosley and me tiptoed right past them, close enough to reach out and touch the table, and the Iguana Gang never knew a thing.

"Did yew hear a noise?" hissed one of the yellows. He cocked his head and listened.

"Smells lak apple juice in here," snarled a black. "Did we hear *whut* noise?"

"Sounded lak tiptoin'," snapped the yellow.

"I ditn't hear nuthin'," sniffed black. "Shut yore mouth an' let us fret."

So they all sat there fretting and flicking their tongues while Crosley and me snuck right by them into the tunnel.

Crosley gave me the flashlight: "Here, ol' man, gimme back the doodad an' turn this on so we can see when we get there."

"Right."

And I held onto Crosley and the flashlight, and Crosley dug his claws in the slick tunnel floor and started climbing, step by step by step.

We knew it was going to be a long way up, because it was a long way down after the rope let loose. And it was too. We even had to stop to put in new flashlight batteries. But Crosley was tough, and he just kept putting one foot in front of another foot, till finally there it was right above us —— the sign for Forbidden Storage Bin Number Seventeen.

We crawled through the side tunnel to the cold green cave.

"Jeeks!" puffed Crosley. *"That* was *work!"* And he stood there staring at the fifty-one thousand and eight pineapple cheesecakes stacked like walls all around us.

"You climb real good," I said, rubbing my whole front side.

Crosley didn't hear me. He kept staring at the pineapple cheesecakes.

"Ut! Ut!" I shoved him: "Hey, Crosley, what did we come up here t' **do,** Crosley?"

"Har?" *Dribble!*

Crosley turned now and blinked, but it was a blank blink, like when you first wake up.

"Har? —————— Oh *Yigg,* John! Was I doin' it again?"

"Yeah, Crosley, you sure were."

He wiped his mouth and turned away from the stacks: "Mighty sorry about that —— Anyhow, hey, come on, let's get started, okay?"

He snapped the I-ain't-here doodad off his belt and gave it to me and we went over to the side tunnel.

"Lemme get this good an' straight," he said. "You're gonna keep the doodad an' wait right here, right? An' I'm gonna crawl out t' the main tunnel an' let 'em hear about it?"

"You got it," I said, but I was frowning anyway: "Listen, how sure are ya about that new whatchamacallit?"

"I ain't never tried it," blinked Crosley.

"Great, thanks for fillin' me in," I muttered. And I stood there and watched him start into the tunnel.

He looked back: "Hang onto the doodad, ol' buddy."

I must've really looked worried: "Be careful, Crosley."

Crosley grinned: "Piece o' chocolate cake. Nothin' but a stroll in the park." Then he gulped loud enough to hear it and was gone.

CHAPTER SEVEN

I was not a happy kid. Not sitting there all alone in that gloomy green cave. And danger or no danger, I was drop-dead tired of the sight and smell of pineapple cheesecakes. I was sitting there shivering in the spooky glow and wishing I was back home in bed, when I heard what had to be the Hog King of Monster Chain Saws start roaring away out in the tunnel. It was so loud it shook some of the pineapple cheesecakes down and they hit the floor and busted —— *Sput! Puh! Putt-Sput!*

"HEY YA BUNCH O' NO GOOD LIZARDS —— ME AN' JOHN'S GOT ALL YOUR NASTY LIZARD FOOD UP HERE, AN' WE'RE KEEPIN' IT TOO. RIGHT, AN' WHAT YA GONNA DO ABOUT THAT, LIZARDS?"

It was Crosley, okay?

AN' DON'T LOOK IN BIN NUMBER SEVENTEEN, NEITHER, AWRIGHT? CAUSE THAT AIN'T WHERE WE'RE HIDIN'!"

And then, with my ears ringing like all, Crosley shot back in the bin beside me like a knotty red torpedo.

"Quick, John, climb on my back an' hold out the doodad!"

I climbed on real quick.

"An' be real quiet," said Crosley.

"Don't worry about me. YOU be quiet."

"Nuff said," said Crosley.

And not five minutes after that, we heard a scuffling, scritching noise off in the tunnel that got louder the closer it got.

"Ya holdin' out the doodad?" whispered Crosley.

"Ya better believe it," I whispered back.

And I held it out even more, and now we could make out voices coming through the side tunnel that sounded mighty mad!

The voices got closer and closer.

"Rat when I wuz fixin' me a snack ⸺ "

"Rat when YEW? Yew must thank yore the onliest one laks Guandoo Puddin'."

75

"Naw, I don't thank thet, but I wuz the first one in the kitchen an' seen everthang gone, rat when the salamander commenced bellerin'."

"Stupid salamander."

"Yeah, an' thet whelp John too."

"Thassrat."

The skins charged in the bin first and stopped and held their noses. Then the yellows busted in and held theirs too, and the blacks right after them.

"Dumb salamander," a skin hissed. "Tryin' t' make us thank he ain't in here!"

"I ain't!" said a chain saw sound.

"Hear thet?" snarled a yellow. "Now we *know* he's in here. He's crazy if he thanks he can trick us, ain't he?"

"Thassrat," smirked the others.

Then they all flicked out their tongues and held their noses and started searching.

"Whut's thet yew said?" a skin hissed at a yellow. They were standing under the big green lamp.

"Nuthin'," snarled yellow. "I ditn't say nuthin'."

"Sounded lak yew said *'Yerk! Yerk!'*" hissed skin.

"Now why would I wawna go an' say a gristle-headed thang lak thet?" snarled yellow.

"Whups me," hissed skin. Then he made a terrible face: *"Wheesh!* Them pineapple cheesecakes shore do stank!"

"Okay," growled a black. "Let's quit all this jab-berin' an' commence ketchin' the big salamander. I'm gettin' sick."

The other black squinted from stack to stack: "Yeah," he snarled. "An' ketch John too."

"Let's do it!" squawked the others. "But let's hurry, okay? These here pineapple cheesecakes stank some-thin' dreadful!"

Then they all held their noses and started search-ing harder than ever.

"Hey John ———"

"Yeah, Crosley?"

"Ya ready?"

"Ready as I'm gonna get."

"Hang on."

"Okay."

And Crosley got up while the iguanas were busy on the other side of the bin, and him and me snuck all the way back out to the main tunnel.

I clicked on the flashlight: "Ya got the thing ready?"

Crosley snapped a little black whatchamacallit off and held it up.

"What is it?" I said. "It looks like a spider."

77

"Better hope it works like one. Okay, lessee quick _____ "

And he took the whatchamacallit and pressed it against the mouth of the side tunnel. And when he pulled it away, some thin black wire stuff came out of it with the end stuck to the tunnel mouth.

"Yerk! Yerk! Yerk!"

Crosley giggled and started pulling the spider thing back and forth and up and down across the opening. And wherever the spider thing touched the wall, the thin wire stuck tight. In just a couple minutes the whole entrance was crisscrossed with the stuff.

"CAN'T FIND US!" Crosley roared into the tunnel.

"Cros! Are ya sure?"

"Feel that," he grinned. "Feel how strong it is."

I grabbed hold of the wire and pushed and pulled, but it wouldn't budge.

"Gosh, it's like the bars in a jail!"

"YERK! YERK! YERK! YERK!" giggled Crosley. " ——— Hey, lissen though, chief, I think I hear 'em comin' now ————— Yeah."

We got quiet and heard the scuffling, scritching noise getting closer. And then the mean voices———

"Bigmouth salamander! We got 'im now fer shore!"

"Yeah, an' thet brat John too!"

Crosley kept on grinning: "Hold your ears a second, John, I'm gonna caterwaul again —— "

And he put his mouth up to the wire and caterwauled for real:

"WHAT'S THE MATTER, LITTLE LIZARDS, YOU AIN'T SCARED, ARE YA? COME ON, ME AN' BIG JOHN ARE OUT HERE WAITIN' FOR YA!"

"LITTLE LIZARDS!" (This iguana voice sounded *super* mad, and it was almost here!) ***"SCEERED? COME ON, GANG, FASTER! LET'S GIT 'EM!"***

And here they came too, the two blacks tearing toward us side by side. Their jaws were open and their teeth were dirty, and right behind them came the skins and yellows as fast as they all could scramble.

Their eyes were gleaming and bright red, but they never saw the spider wire.

"SALAMANDER STEW!" the blacks squalled. ***"AN' JOHN STEW TOO!"***

When all at once **KRiNK!** —— just like ***THAT!*** they hit the wire and stopped. They crumpled back down on the tunnel floor, and the skins who were right behind them and couldn't stop went **PRiNK!**

the same way. And then **KRiNK-KRUNK!** the yellows did too, one right after the other.

They all landed on top of each other and made the silliest looking iguana pile in the world!

"*Yerk! Yerk! Yerk! Yerk! Yerk!* went Crosley. "*Yerk! Yerk! Yerk! Yerk!*"

I peeked in through the wire: "Are they dead, Cros?"

They did look like it, all piled up and nobody moving.

"Naw," said Crosley. "This crew's too nasty t' kill so easy. Hang on, they probly ain't even hurt bad."

And sure enough, after a minute a couple of them wiggled. And then the others woke up one at a time and stirred and growled.

"*Hey, git off us, yew scumbags!*" snarled the blacks on the bottom of the pile. "*Git off, yew copperbacks!*"

The yellows groaned and rolled down off the top.

"Aww!"

"Yow!"

"Ow!"

Then the skins got off too, till finally all six iguanas stood there sore and blinking their red eyes and wondering what in the world had happened.

A black pointed at a yellow: "Hey, liverlips, yew really look stupid. Just lookit yoreself —— "

"*Me?*" pointed yellow. "How bout *yew,* hawg breath? Yore a fine one t' say *anybody* looks stupid!"

Then the whole gang looked at each other, and they were stamped all over with millions of tiny little lines from running into the wire so hard! They looked just like iguana spider webs!

"*Yerk! Yerk! Yerk! Yerk!*" cackled Crosley.

"*Hey,*" hissed black, "*rat here's the salamander!*"

"*Shutup, salamander,*" squawked the skins.

"*Hey, let's git 'im!*" yelled the rest.

And they charged straight at Crosley and me again, and the yellows who were in front went **SPRUNK!** right into the spider wire again and bounced back on top of the blacks and skins!

I giggled: "Hey, it serves ya right, lizards!"

"Shutup, John," growled a black, and then a yellow too: "Shutup, banjo-eyes!"

The whole gang was back in a big heap.

"I'll talk if I want to —— Hey, listen, Crosley, ya sure they can't get out?"

"No way, buddy. They couldn't get through that stuff with a bulldozer."

First the yellows, and then the skins scrambled up and grabbed the wire, and they pushed and pulled and grunted and shoved and got madder and madder, but they couldn't do diddley.

"Crenwinkle calls it his trap-spinner loblolly," Crosley chuckled. "Him an' me thought we might run into the iguanas on some Program, so he invented it for us."

"Crinwankle!" screeched the iguanas. ***"We mighta knowed it!"***

"Him an' his dumb inventions!" squawked a black down on the floor. ***Erp!***

"Birdbrain Crinwankle!" squalled the other black.

"You crooks oughta be so birdbrained," said Crosley. "Cause then maybe ya wouldn't be in the fix you're in."

"Let us out, Crawzly," sniffed the first black. *"Shew,* it smells *so* nasty."

They were all starting to look more and more sick and less and less mad.

"Yeah, John, how bout it?" whined a skin. He sniffed the air and made an awful face.

"We won't even trouble yew no more neither," gulped the yellows.

They were staggering back and forth and turning more and more the color of cold bacon grease.

"Sorry," said Crosley. "You schmucks got yourselves into this by thievin', an' now you're right where ya belong."

Some of the iguanas were holding their throats now, and the others were grabbing their bellies.

"Please let us out, Crawzly," they whined. "Them pineapple cheesecakes stank worse'n anythang alive!"

"Stink?" said Crosley. He sniffed: "Smells mighty appetizin' t' me. You smell any stink, John?"

"Not exactly stink, Cros, but it's what gave me the whole idea. I mean if I was gettin' so tired o' pineapple cheesecakes, I figured what if the iguanas —— "

The skins snatched hold of the wire: **"Lissen,**

John ——— "

Erp! ——— One let go and grabbed his mouth.

"Lissen," begged the other: **"Okay, yew got us good this time. We'll do anythang yew say. Just let us git away from them there pineapple stankheaps an' we'll slide back down the Loot Chute an' won't bother nobody no more!"**

"Yerk! Yerk!" cackled Crosley. "Izzat so?"

"Oh yeah, we swear!" hollered the whole gang together.

I was shaking my head: "I don't believe 'em, Crosley."

"Me neither, John ——— **So okay, ol' buddy,"** he winked, **"let's us just get on back up where we came from an' leave 'em in there. Get on my shoulders now** ——— "

We started up the tunnel.

"Naw, naw," squalled all six voices. **"Naw, we'll git stunk all t' flinders!"**

" ——— **Don't, Crawzly! Please, Crawzly!"**

" ——— **Please, John! Don't do it!"**

" ——— **I thank I'm gonna throw up!"**

" ——— **Me too!"**

GRAK!

"Yerk! Yerk! —— "

"Button up," I whispered.

" —— Yk!"

Us two Night Buddies had gone just a little way up the tunnel and stopped.

"Let's let 'em worry a little while longer," whispered Crosley. *"Then we'll see."*

"Just what I was gonna say," I whispered back.

The iguanas got sicker and sicker. And the sicker they got, the scareder they got.

One after the other one was yelling:

" —— I gotta throw up agin!"

" —— Then git away from me!"

" —— Aw Crawzly, please!"

" —— Crawzly's left, jackass!"

" —— Aw my garsh! Aw naw, naw, naw!"

" —— Crawzly an' John's gone an' left us in here!"

Bork!

" —— Why did we have t' go an' steal all these nasty stankpies is whut I wawna know!"

" —— It wudn't my dumb idear!"

" —— Mine neither!"

" —— It wuz yew yeller bellies who thought

it up!"

    " —— Wudn't neither! It wuz them skinbacks rat there!"

    " —— Not us, slimelips!"

ERP!

    " —— Aw, I want Mawma!"

    " —— I want 'er too!"

    " —— So do all the rest of us!"

    " —— MAWMAAAA!"

GRAK!

CHAPTER EIGHT

"*Okay, John, let's ease back down t' the side tunnel an' have another discussion with 'em,*" whispered Crosley.

"*Right, buddyroo. But hey, how're we ever gonna let 'em out? An' us get away, I mean?*"

"*That's the easy part,*" grinned Crosley. And he pulled his claws back and let us down till we could see in through the spider wire.

The iguanas were in rough shape. They were laying all along the tunnel with their eyes shut and their tongues hanging out on the floor. Some were holding their bellies, and the others were grabbing their mouths or their throats. Nobody moved much. There were just little growls and groans, and every now and then the evil sound of one of those bums hurling lunch.

We watched for a minute, and then Crosley leaned back and bellowed:

"HEY, LIZARDS, YA KNOW WHAT YA LOOK LIKE? YA LOOK LIKE BIG PUDDLES O' COLD BACON GREASE!"

"Whuf? Whut's thet?"

GORP!

The iguanas wiggled a little.

"YEAH," roared Crosley, **"AN' YA STINK LIKE OL' SWEATY UNDERSHIRTS IN AUGUST!"**

One of the yellows lifted his head real slow.

"Hey," he croaked. *"It's Crawzly! Crawzly's back!"*

"Crawzly?" gulped the other yellow.

"Yeah, him an' good ol' John! They're rat here outside the wires!"

"HOORAY!" hollered a skin, climbing over the other skin and clapping.

"Let us out, Crawzly!" screeched two or three of them.

"Yeah, John, thet's whut yew come for, ain't it, John?"

Crosley blinked: "I don't understand none o' this."

"Whut yew mean?" squawked the yellow next to

the wire.

"*Yerk! Yerk!* I mean, I don't understand why anybody'd wanna get away from a cave full o' pineapple cheesecakes. Why if it was me, I'd just go in there an' grab me ten or twelve an' ——"

"WE'LL GIVE 'EM TO YA!" squalled the whole gang together. **"JUST LET US OUTTA HERE AN' YEW CAN TAKE BACK EVER SINGLE PINEAPPLE CHEESECAKE WE STOLE!"**

"Mmmm? Ya don't say? That's an interestin' offer, John, ain't it?"

I looked in at them: "It sure is. That's a whole lot o' pineapple cheesecakes."

Crosley winked at me and then spoke up real loud: " —— *Yeah, that's just the trouble, though. All them pineapple cheesecakes! Why, it'd take me an' John three weeks past next month t' haul all that outta here.*"

He winked at me again, then looked in: "Naw, lizards, we ain't gonna do it. You'll just have t' stay in there forever, I guess."

When Crosley said this, the iguanas all blorfed at once. It was a terrible noise, sort of like a bomb exploding inside a tankful of greasy water. Crosley and me scrambled up the tunnel till it stopped.

Then Crosley peeked back in through the wire: "What's the matter, lizards, did I say somethin' t' upset your tummies?"

The iguanas could barely stand up or even speak.

"Crawzly, please —— " croaked the closest yellow. *"Please just let us outta here rat now an' we'll put ever one o' the nasty thangs back where we got 'em from our own selves! Yew won't have t' do nuthin'! Just please let us out rat now!"*

Crosley looked at me and scratched his head ——

"What d'ya think, buddy? Ya think that's a fair deal or what d'ya think?"

"I dunno. What if they don't keep their promise?"

"That's right. Okay, lizards, so how do we know ya'll do what ya say ya will?"

"Yore lookin' at why," groaned the yellow. "Cain't yew see we'd do anythang —— **ANYTHANG** —— if we knew we'd never have t' smell one o' these here pineapple dreckpies no more?"

I shined the flashlight in the iguana's red eyes. The batteries were getting weak again: "How can ya stand carryin' all those pineapple cheesecakes up out o' here, then?"

"That's right," said Crosley. "How bout that?"

The yellows spluttered: "We got stank masks. It's how we got the thangs put up in the bins in the first place."

"Fine," said Crosley. "So how can we be sure ya won't just decide t' leave an' forget t' put everything back where ya stole it from?"

A black dragged himself up to the wire: "Thet's simple," he croaked. "There ain't but one way out. The way yew an' John come down, Crawzly."

"Yew could guard the hole easy," groaned a yellow.

Black tried to say something, but both skins rushed up and jerked him and yellow away. They snatched hold of the wire.

"This here is our HOME!" they squealed. ***"We don't WAWNA leave it!"***

Crosley looked at me and I looked at Crosley.

"Sounds pretty good t' me," I said.

"Yeah," said Crosley. "Awright." He turned to the iguanas: "Me an' John have decided t' take ya up on your offer. But I'm warnin' ya about one thing right now ——"

" —— Yeah, Crawzly?"

" —— *Shore, Crawzly!*"

" —— *Whut, Crawzly?*" shrieked everybody.

"If them pineapple cheesecakes ain't all put back in the factory three days from tomorra mornin', I'm gonna go t' the Jellybean Factory myself, an' the Lizard Cheese Factory an' see to it that ya don't *get* no more lizard cheese an' jellybeans! Do ya understand that real good, lizards?"

" —— *Yeah, Crawzly!*"

" —— *We shore do, Crawzly!*"

" —— *Don't yew worry, Crawzly!*" screeched the iguanas.

"An' another thing," he said. "If them pineapple cheesecakes ain't stacked up real tidy after ya *do* bring 'em back, I'm gonna get a big ol' fan an' I'm gonna aim it down your hole an' blow all the pineapple cheesecake smell right back down t' where ya live at! Ya understand that too, lizards?"

The iguanas shut their eyes and shivered just thinking about it. "We understand," they gulped.

"Okay, then," said Crosley. "Big John, ya ready t' start home?"

"Man," I said, "you nailed that one good."

"Hey, John an' Crawzly," yelled one of the skins,

"hang on a second! Tell us where yew hid the jelly-beans an' lizard cheese we awready had!"

"Yeah," squeaked the other one. *"But first will yew please tell us how t' git out!"*

"CROSLEY," I yelled, "THERE'S SMOKE COMIN' UP THE TUNNEL!"

"SHNORF!" went Crosley. "YOU'RE RIGHT! SOMETHIN' MUSTA CAUGHT ON FIRE DOWN THERE!"

"Yeah," I sniffed, *"I wonder what it is!"*

"Sure stinks, don't it?" snorted Crosley.

The iguanas were sniffing and snorting too.

"AW NAW, NAW, NAW!" one of them screamed. *"IT'S OUR JELLYBEANS AN' LIZARD CHEESE!"*

"YORE RAT!" yelled another one.

"THIS IS TURRIBLE!" hollered a third one. *"AW NAW, NAW, NAW!"*

Crosley looked in at them: "How could this o' happened? I mean me an' John stuffed it all up the chimley. That part was my idea."

"YEW CAKEBRAINED SALAMANDER!" squalled three iguanas. *"WE STARTED A FAR IN THE FARPLACE RAT BEFORE WE CHASED YEW UP HERE!"*

"IT WUZ GITTIN' CHILLY!" squeaked another one.

"YEW SIMPLEMINDED SALAMANDER!" squawked

two more.

"AT EASE, AT EASE!" barked Crosley. "Hold it down, lizards. Me an' John'll slide back down an' put the fire out."

"AIRHEADED SALAMANDER!" hollered all six. *"EVERTHANG'S RURNT BY NOW! WHO IN THE WORLD EVER HEERED O' SMOKED JELLYBEANS, FOR CRYIN' OUT LOUD? OR LIZARD CHEESE FONDOO!"*

"Besides," snarled a black, "the sprinkler system'll put the stupid far out."

Crosley looked around real sudden: *"SPRINKLER SYSTEM?"*

"Shore," smirked black. "Whut yew thank them little pipes rat there's for, runnin' all up an' down the tunnel?"

Crosley and me knew the answer now. We looked right beside us at the pipes and saw all these tiny holes in them, like in a shower spout. Crosley was starting to lose his red.

"Hey, lissen, lizards, that thing ain't gonna spray water all over, is it? I mean like way up here away from the fire?" He was pink already and starting to shake.

"Shore it's gonna spray way up here," snarled the same old black. "Soon as it smells smoke, it cuts loose all over everplace."

"All the way up the tunnel?" gulped Crosley.

"All the way t' the top," hissed black. "It ain't perticler."

Crosley peeked around at the pipes again: **"How long ya guess before it starts?"**

"Any ol' second now," sniffed the same old black-shirted iguana. "Soon as thet smoke gits t' the smoke-smeller box rat over my bed."

"THEN GRAB ON TIGHT, JOHN! WE GOTTA SHAG OUR KEESTERS OUTTA HERE!"

I barely had time to drop the flashlight and grab onto Crosley before the two of us were tearing up the slippery tunnel even faster than we had slid down when the rope came loose. Crosley's little legs were spinning away like eggbeaters and it was black dark and I could feel the air rushing past my face.

"Gotta make time!" panted Crosley. **"Wuff! Gotta make time!"**

We barely heard the voices down below us ——

" —— Crawzly, wait, how d'we git out?"

" —— Crawzly!"

Crosley slowed down just long enough to yell back through the dark:

"Just lay there, lizards! The wire'll melt itself in twenny minutes!"

The voices sounded even teenier now as we scrambled up the tunnel ——

"Tomater-twatted salamander!"

"Wish we'd o' knowed thet!"

"Git offa me!"

"Move yore own self!"

HiLGE!

Crosley didn't hear any of it: *"Gotta make time!"* he huffed. *"Gotta get gone!"*

I held on and remembered about him and water, which was why we were racing up the tunnel in such a hurry! We were way too far up now to hear the iguanas' snarls.

"Hey, C-Crosley —— "

"Fwuf! —— What, buddy?"

"Listen, don't ya think we oughta have your p-pills ready? It can't be far now, but I mean just in case?"

"Sharp thinkin', buddy —— Wurf! —— Lemme get 'em out."

"Cros, wait, be careful —— "

But Crosley was already reaching inside his jacket and scrambling as fast as he could on his three other legs.

"Here, John, hang onto 'em."

"Cros, slow down, you're g-gonna —— "

It happened right then. The pill bottle squirted right through Crosley's claws, and I grabbed at it and just missed and the lid popped off, and the lid and the bottle and about nine hundred little black pills scattered off down the tunnel.

"Uh-oh," I said.

"Uh-oh is right," said Crosley. *"We gotta get out now or I'll be doin' the Black Bottom till —— Woof! —— till lunch time next Tuesday!"*

"It's okay, Cros, we're gonna make it —— "

"GOTTA make it! ———— Hey, lissen, maybe I ____ "

"May-maybe ya what?"

"I think maybe I see it!" wuffed Crosley.

"The top?"

"Fwoo! —— Yeah, I can just see a teeny speck way up there. I think maybe we ARE gonna make it!"

"Before the sprinkler st-starts?"

Clack! *"I'm sure gonna give it a try, ol' trouper!"*

And when he said that, Crosley put his head down and stuck his tail straight out in back and climbed even faster! His claws made real sparks through the slippery goo, and it was all I could do to stay on him!

"Gotta make time —— Wuff!"

I looked up now and saw it myself. It was still way up there, the speck, but it got bigger, and still bigger. And then I could make out that it was square like the tunnel and —— Right, it sure was! It was the hole in the factory floor and we were almost there!

"EXCELSIOR!" shouted Crosley, his little legs whirling and whirling. We were just two ticks from the top now!

"EXCELS ——"

—— *SPLUSH!*

A huge wave of cold water caught us smack in the face! It wasn't any sprinkler water either; it was enough to soak a cow in, and it came down on us from the top of the tunnel!

Crosley and me were drenched!

But drenched or dry, we scrambled up on the factory floor, and there stood Big Foot Mae looking all amazed and astounded. I mean her mouth was hanging as wide open as the big empty wash tub she had in her hands!

CHAPTER NINE

As soon as I could scramble off him (Wow, I had dents all over my whole front!) Crosley started bouncing up and down on the factory floor trying to get his clothes off.

"John, buddy, I'm in for it now!" he hollered.

"Geez, Cros——"

He was bouncing like a basketball and trying to unzip his pants. He finally jumped out of them, and the pants with all of the whatchamacallits clattered on the floor.

Crosley was naked now, and super wet, and his color was back. But it wasn't red color anymore—— it was plain old crocodile green!

He never slowed down, though. He slapped his

left back leg and stomped forward on it. He slapped his right one and did the same. He clapped. And he started singing too, that is if you believe chain saws can do stuff like that.

♪ **"Jump right down an' then ya wriggle back, Slip t' the left an' slide t' the right ⸺ "** ♩♩

He looked trapped and awful unhappy as he stomped his left back leg forward again and slapped his right, stomped his right forward and slapped his left and clapped ⸺

♩ **"Hands on your hips an' mess all around, Shimmy an' shake till ya hit the ground, That's the sure enough Black Bottom."** ♪♩

Big Foot Mae had put her wash tub down and was starting to boogie along with Crosley ⸺

"Ya silly whale!" yelled Crosley. *"Turn your back! An' go get us some towels!"*

Mae quit boogieing: "Sorry, man, I'll get 'em for ya directly." And she thudded over to a cabinet on the wall that said *GUEST TOWELS.*

♪ **"Ol' Black Bottom make ya scrooch your** ♩ ♪
   feet ⸺ "

Crosley was doing it all over the factory now ⸺
slapping his hips beside the big mixer, clapping and
stomping by the oven houses, and when giant Mae
came back with the towels trying real hard not to look,
he was jerking his knees up and down next to a big
heap of Puzzle pieces that had fallen off the Ceiling.

"Started down the road an' it went t'
France ————
(Thanks, Big Foot. Give John one too!)"

Crosley Black Bottomed round and round the Puzzle pile and tried to dry himself at the same time. That's when I pulled my shoes off and thought I saw something inside the one with the rubber band.

 "It's got me an' Big Foot in a trance ————
(You too, buddy, take your clothes off an' get dry!)"

"I'm *doin'* it, Crosley —— *Hey Crosley, here's two pills! They musta fell in my shoe!*"
"Gimme! Hey, gimme 'em!"
"Right!"
"Hand 'em here!"
I got the pills to him just as he bounced again, and he slapped them in his mouth on the way back down.
"Thanks, buddy! Woo, what a relief THAT is!"
I wrapped up in my towel and worried anyway: "Hey, Crosley, are ya really gonna get okay, do ya think?"

"Not a problem, buddy! —— *Wuff!* —— *Pills never failed me yet!"*

"It's a dog," he sang,
"That ol' Black Bottom Dance —— **"**

"Hey, your red's comin' back," I said after a minute.

"That's right," said Mae. "I can see it myself."

Crosley stomped and looked down at himself. He tied his towel around him and grinned: *"Means the pills're kickin' in."* But he kept right on slapping his hips and clapping and jerking his knees up and down. *"Shouldn't be long now!"* he hollered.

And sure enough, while Mae and me stood there watching him jump all over the place, Crosley turned a little less green, and a little more red, and he started slowing down too, so that by the time he got to be dark pink, he was hardly jumping around at all.

Finally, exactly two minutes after taking the pills, he got his bright old red back and stopped!

"EXCELSIOR!" he let out with, and crumpled down to rest.

Mae rumbled over to him: "I'm sorry as I can be about all that water, Crosley, but smoke was comin' up outta the hole. An' I didn't know you was already on the way up."

"Please don't lose any hairs over it," breathed Crosley. "Hey, John buddy, are ya dry? Are ya warm enough?"

"I'm fine," I said. "But our clothes aren't so hot."

"Not t' fret," chirped Mae. "I'll put 'em in the Number Two Oven-House. Have 'em dry in no time."

"Mm," said Crosley. "You just do that, then. I gotta rest."

Mae put the clothes in to dry and came back: "So tell me right out —— How'd things go down yonder? I sure hope you was able t' get the problem fixed."

"Funny ya should ask," growled Crosley. "How come ya let go o' the rope? Ya like t' fixed all me an' John's problems right there!"

Big Mae looked sorry: "I got t' ask your pardon about that too," she said. "But listen a minute. I was settin' right there by the hole, settin', listenin', an' holdin' on just like you said, when all at once —— "

She pointed to a jagged white gap in the Ceiling above the Puzzle heap.

" —— All at once that whole section o' Puzzle

fell down, an' it scared me so, it's a wonder I didn't jump right down the hole on top o' you!"

"That woulda been a tall wonder," growled Crosley.

"Hey, ya know what?" I said. "I bet you're usin' the wrong kinda glue."

"It weren't that," said the giant woman. "Did you look at these pieces here on the floor?" (She picked up a handful and showed them to us.) "These, you mighta noticed, go t' the Great Wet Dog Constellation."

"The Great Wet *What?*" said Crosley, starting to get up.

"The Great Wet Dog Constellation. The big dot on this piece here, see it? That's ol' Grandaddy Goosehound Hisownself!"

Crosley squinted at the Puzzle piece: "Yeah, fine," he said. "But what's that got t' do with the cost o' razzberry flapjacks?"

"A whole lot," said Mae. "If you'll just stop an' think a minute what it is wet dogs do."

"Whazzat? What izzit wet dogs do?"

"Hey," I said, "I know. They *shake!* Ain't that right, Mae?"

"Don't say 'ain't,'" frowned Crosley.

I stuck my tongue out at him.

"Yeah, but he's right!" said Mae. "They *do* shake! They're *bound* t' shake! An' what I'm thinkin' is, these pieces just shook theirselves right down off the Ceilin'!"

Crosley looked up at the ragged hole: "Ya don't mean t' say?"

"Do too. But now I can't figure out how t' get 'em t' stay back *up* there."

"Use screws," I said, standing there in my towel.

Mae whirled around: *"Say what?"*

"Use screws," I said. "That'll let the glue dry better too."

Mae shot Crosley a look of giant woman joy and Crosley fired her back a ninety-nine tooth grin.

"Why, that's it!" squealed Mae. *"The boy's right —— Screws!"*

"Yerk! Yerk! Yerk! Yerk!"

An' if ya use black ones, they won't show either," I said.

"That's it!" yipped Mae. *"That's the answer!"*

"Yerk! Yerk! Yerk! Yerk!"

Mae looked down at the pieces and back up at the Ceiling and smiled and smiled.

"We got the crooks t' quit too," I said.

Big Foot Mae wasn't listening. She was too busy thinking about her Great Wet Dog Constellation.

"Right," I kept trying to tell her. "An' they're gonna bring back all the pineapple cheesecakes they stole an' —— **HEY MAE!**"

"Hm? Say what?" She turned and blinked: "Excuse me there, big guy, did you say somethin'?"

Crosley jumped in: "John just said we solved the problem ya reported t' Headquarters, Mae. You're back in business. What's the matter, ya got glue in your ears too?"

"Glue?" Mae stuck a finger in her ear. "Naw —— *Oh, hey, man, gimme a break!* Ya say ya did straighten out the pineapple cheesecake mess, though, right?"

"We straightened it out," grumbled Crosley.

"That's real fine," said Mae. She was studying a piece of Great Wet Dog Puzzle between her fingers. "Hey, look here, how do ya think a screw would fit in right here next t' these Houndog Stars?"

"Just really first-rate," snorted Crosley. "Hey, lissen, Big Foot, me an' John're kinda tired after all the stuff we been doin', so would ya mind goin' over an' findin' out if our clothes're dry? We gotta snatch some Zs sometime or other."

"Well just look at me!" squeaked Mae. "Here I am bein' so rude!" And she put down her Houndog Stars and went straight over and brought us back our clothes. "Here," she said, "they're dry an' warm, an' as soon as ya get 'em on I'll take ya straight t' the station. That is, unless —— "

"Unless what? Har?" Crosley looked suspicious.

"Unless," said Mae, "you'll wait an' let me fix you a little somethin' t' carry along."

"What sorta somethin'?" squinted Crosley.

"*Ut!* I bet *I* know! You mean pineapple cheese-cakes, don't ya, Mae?"

She just smiled.

"Izzat it?" yelped Crosley. **"Izzit? Izzat what ya mean, Mae?"**

Mae nodded.

"Well aw*right* then! Now that's what I call a real world-class idea! Ain't that a world-class idea, John?"

"I guess it probly is," I sighed. "If it doesn't take real long."

"Real long —— ? Oh yeah, that's right. Awright, Mae, so how long's it gonna take? Not long, right? Not long at all, I bet."

"Not accordin' t' my mind," said Mae. "Only

three minutes an' two seconds if we speed Jones up."

So Crosley and me got dressed, and Mae took out her oilcan and clumped along the machine squirting oil in where little signs said **SQUIRT SOME RIGHT HERE.** Then she got to the big mixer where a handle was sticking out of the side. She flipped the handle from **REGULAR SPEED** to **URGENT SPEED: PINEAPPLE CHEESECAKES IN JUST THREE MINUTES AND TWO SECONDS FLAT.**

"Awright," she said. "Crosley, if you'll just start Jones over there —— "

Crosley looked way up the wall at the brown button: *"Me? You must be kiddin'! I ain't no giraffe!"*

"Aw, there I go," said Mae, thumping across the factory. "I keep forgettin' why I *have* this job —— "

She reached way up over the door and pushed the button, and as soon as she did the sweet humming sound started and the belt moved, but much faster than last time. The pineapple cheesecake stuff popped up on it and scooted straight into the big mixer, and Crosley ran over and watched the aluminum pie pans with graham cracker crusts getting filled up.

CLACK! *Drool!*

Jones worked really fast, and when the pans went in the first little oven-house, it was hardly any time before they popped out on the other side all hot.

"Crosley!" I yelled. *"You're slobberin' on the floor again!"*

CLACK!

He looked down: "Yeah, buddy, you're mighty right —— "

And he took out his handkerchief and held it against his mouth and watched the pans getting squirted with pineapple and sugar and all the other stuff. And when they went in the second oven-house, Crosley hurried down to watch them come out. His handkerchief was soaked and couldn't hold the drool anymore, and he was splashing up and down from excitement in his own puddle.

I ran and slid both our towels under him and Mae waited over by the wall buttons.

And then, just when I was going over to get more towels, the oven-house popped open and out came a brand-new pineapple cheesecake, sweet and steamy and followed by another one just like it, and another one, and another one, till finally forty-four of them had slid by Crosley's nose and gone off to where the tops and boxes were.

Mae pushed the **_NO PINEAPPLE CHEESECAKES_** button and hurried over, and Crosley's mouth was raining down like a carwash.

"Listen," she said: *"If you'd rather eat 'em here _____ "*

Crosley didn't even look at her. He snatched the two pans closest to him and flipped the insides right in his mouth. Then he pitched away the pans, grabbed two more and flipped their insides in too and ——

"Mind, they're hot —— " yelped Mae.

Crosley blew out a mouthful of steam, grinned big, and gulped. He popped in two more panfuls and gulped again.

"ExCELSiOR!" he sighed, and blinked his eyes at the stars in the great Ceiling. And then, with Mae and me all amazed, Crosley went along the belt, and with no help from anywhere, he stood on his back feet and swallowed all but nine of the whole world's output of pineapple cheesecakes for that hour of that night.

Two at a time too. And it didn't take him quite three minutes and two seconds.

He was reaching for more when a button popped off his yellow jacket and I yelled: **"Crosley, your belly!"**

"Har?"

He looked down. And it was a good thing too, because his middle had blown up as big as a beach-ball and pushed his jacket way up under his front legs, and his pants, well, his pants looked ready to pop open and head the other way any second.

Crosley backed off, fell back on his backside, and burped —— **BA-GROOP!**

He grinned up at me: "Right, buddy, thanks. That's probly enough for right now."

He stumbled up and felt his belly.

"Yeah, that snack went down real fine. Say Mae, you got one o' them boxes an' some tops I can use for the rest o' these? A few more'll go great right when I hit the sack."

"Sure do," said Mae. She went and got the things. "I wasn't sure you'd need these for a minute there."

"Much obliged," said Crosley. He boxed up the last nine pineapple cheesecakes.

" —— So what d'ya think, John? Think we should cruise on outta here now or what?"

YES! I nodded. (Several times!)

"'Then I'm way in front o' ya," said Mae. "If you'll just follow me on out t' the van."

"Sounds like a plan," I yawned.

Mae got to the door, then turned and looked back: "Just a half a second," she said, clumping over to the pile of Great Wet Dog pieces. She picked one up and looked at it, put it down again, and clumped back. She opened the door and let us out in the dark.

"Sorry about that," she said when we climbed in the van. "That piece with the White Wolfhounds, it's white all over, just about, an' I had t' see if there was enough black for a screw not t' show."

Crosley shut his door: "I thought ya mighta got hungry. *Yerk! Yerk!*"

I turned to Mae. (We were both in the back seat!) "Ya know what, ya didn't need t' worry about that, Mae."

She backed the van out in the street: "Is that so, curlytop? Why not?"

I yawned again: "Ya just get some white screws when ya get the black ones. That way ya can use white screws in the white places, an' black screws in the black places."

The gigantic woman turned and looked right at me: "Son," she said: "If you ain't a credit t' the Night Buddies, I musta missed out. Crosley, your boy's gonna do fine!" She stepped on the gas and started us off.

"Aw, quit now —— " I said.

BA-GROOP! blurched Crosley when we hit a big bump. *"Yerk! Yerk! Yerk!"* *(GRUP!)*

CHAPTER TEN

The streets were all dark and empty, so it didn't take Mae and me and Crosley long to drive to the station. Mae got out and went with us down to the token booth.

"No foolin'," she said. "I sure hope you'll come back an' see my Sky before very long. Now that I'm able t' work on it —— "

Crosley grinned and hugged his pineapple cheesecake box: "Yeah, we just might can arrange that. Hey lissen, though, did I tell ya them iguanas are bringin' back all your other pineapple cheesecakes?"

"No, Crosley, ya didn't," I said. "I told her, remember? We'll see ya soon, Mae, okay? An' if the pineapple cheesecakes aren't all put back neat, you just call Crenwinkle."

Huge Mae reached down with her one-fingered glove and shook my hand: "Thank you, Brother John. Thank you so much."

"Not a problem," I said. "Hey, tell me somethin' quick before the train comes —— "

"Sure thing."

"How come they call ya Big Foot? Your feet don't look any bigger than the rest of ya."

Mae chuckled: "They don't look no smaller, do they?"

"Nope."

"Then they must be big, right?" And she winked at me and waved goodbye and rumbled up the stairs in her graham cracker coveralls with pineapples all over them.

Crosley snapped the I-D gimcrack off and looked in the window of the token booth.

There was a tiny little orange-haired woman in there asleep.

"Two tokens, willya please? Night Buddies —— "

The little woman SNORKED once and pushed the tokens out without even waking up. "Keep the change," she gurgled in her sleep.

"Much obliged," said Crosley. We pushed through the turnstiles and headed out on the platform when suddenly ——

"AT EATHE!"

Whatever it was sounded more like a great big train on the tracks than a voice ——

"ALLWIGHT, WHO'TH THE WITHEGUY AS BWOUGHT THE CHAIN THAW IN HERE!"

Crosley turned and pointed at himself: "Ya mean me, lady?"

"YER DARN TOOTIN' I MEAN YOU, CWOCKODILE!" roared the little head.

"YOU KNOW CHAIN THAWS AIN'T ALLOWED IN THITH ————— Oh."

The freight train voice died away.

Crosley giggled: "You were sayin', lady?"

The tiny little woman was cool. She gummed him back this huge toothless grin and fluttered her fingers goodbye.

We waved back, and right when we did, we heard our train coming, the *NIGHT FOLKS EXPRESS* this time. It clattered in and opened its doors, and Crosley and me got on.

The car was empty except for one old night-watchman in a blue nightwatchman's suit. We sat down across from him and the train started with a jerk.

"Why John and Crosley!" he said. "How congenial! So what sort of Program did you two gents have?"

"Not too bad," said Crosley. "How about yourself?"

"Really top drawer," said the nightwatchman. "I saw every single thing that went on in my Sector! First time I've done it in weeks."

"Izzat so?" said Crosley. "Hey lissen, Watchman, lemme tell ya what me an' John done. We went over t' the Pineapple Cheese —— "

"*Crosley!*"

"Har?"

"Chill, Crosley. We rescued a whole bunch o' dessert, Watchman."

"Yeah, that's right, Watchman. Say, it's sure nice commutin' with ya."

"It's always nice commuting with the two of *you,*" said the old man. "Oh, by the way, Crosley, aren't you neglecting something?"

"Har? What ya talkin' about?"

"Aren't you going to give John his orange shoelaces?"

"Well dump me down the downspout if you ain't dead right, Watchman! Here, buddy —— "

He reached in his pocket and gave me the ones he got in the drugstore.

"Right, thanks," I said. I snapped the rubber band off my shoe and laced it up. Then I switched the laces in the other shoe.

The train was going fast now, rattling past block after block of dark buildings. When it slowed down, the nightwatchman got up.

I waved: "Nice commutin' with ya, night fella!"

"Let's do it again soon," smiled the old man.

Crosley waved too, and when the train stopped and the nightwatchman got off, I saw that he had the same bright orange shoelaces in his dark blue shoes!

We started going again, and Crosley stretched out and yawned.

"Hey John, lissen, tell me when we go back underground, will ya? I'm gonna rest my eyes for just a second."

"Sure, Cros."

I kept watch out the window. When we went in the tunnel, I poked him.

"SNERK! HAR?" Crosley's eyes popped open and he looked all around.

"What izzit, buddy?"

"We're back underground. Ya said t' wake ya up."

"For real?" blinked Crosley.

"Look," I said, pointing at all the black outside.

"Hey, neat," he said. "I wasn't asleep, though, ya know that, right?"

"You were snorin'."

"Says who?"

"They coulda heard ya a long way off."

Crosley blinked, then grinned and sat up and looked out the window. We flashed by several lit-up subway stations and kept going. The next one was our stop.

Crosley peeked inside his pineapple cheesecake box: " —— seven, eight, nine. Yeah, they're all in here." (He closed the box back up.) "Lissen, ol' man, I'd like ya t' take a couple o' these for yourself. When we get back t' your place."

I made a face: "No thanks, Cros. I don't think I wanna see anymore pineapple cheesecakes for a pretty long time."

Crosley brightened up: "Ya sure?"

"Yeah, I'm real sure."

And then the train slowed down. It rumbled into the 83rd Street Station and stopped and the doors slid open, and me and Crosley got off.

We crossed the platform to the stairs, and when we did we passed the same squatty little man with his big dead cigar in the token booth.

"Hey, Night Buddies, see ya next Program!" he yelled.

I waved, but Crosley couldn't wave because he was carrying the box. He grinned big, though, and winked two or three times.

We went up the stairs to the sidewalk. There wasn't anybody else around this late at night. We walked along for a couple blocks and passed the all-night drugstore that sold shoelaces and flashlight batteries. I waved to the cash register woman with the purple lipstick still sitting in there and she waved back.

"That reminds me," said Crosley. "I gotta get me a new flashlight after I drop you off."

I looked over at him, then shoved my hands in my pockets and kept walking. "Yeah, I guess ya do, don't ya. I hadn't thought o' that."

"Ya don't miss much," said Crosley. "Ya know, I guess you're just about the sharpest Night Buddy I ever had. If ya want the straight scoop, I mean."

"I had a real good time," I said, staring down at the sidewalk.

We were nearly there now, and I guess Crosley noticed me dragging along ——

"Somethin' wrong, buddy? What ya lookin' so sad about?"

I poked along till we got right to my steps. Then I turned and looked right at him ——

"Crosley, can I ask ya somethin'?"

Crosley set his box right down on the sidewalk: "Now what d'ya mean by that? *Sure* ya can ask me somethin'. Ask me anything ya want."

I toed the sidewalk with my hands in my pockets: "Crosley, I just got t' know before ya leave —— Are ya ever gonna —— I mean, when are ya gonna come back, Crosley?"

Crosley cocked his head sideways: "Hey, I don't get it, John. I mean, didn't I tell ya about how the Night Buddies operates?"

"No," I said, "I guess ya didn't."

"Y¡GG!" said Crosley, and he reached out and

slapped himself right on the nose! "No *wonder* ya had t' ask me! Well *sure* I'm gonna come back, buddy! I'm gonna come back every night when ya really can't sleep. Just like I done tonight. Jeeks, that's what the Night Buddies is all *about,* John!"

"Well *okay,*" I grinned, and this grin was a twenty-four tooth one if you could see all the way in back. And twenty-four teeth is as big as grins get when you're my age. I'm pretty sure about that.

"Well utterly out*standin',*" said Crosley. "Awright, now that we got *that* straightened out, why don't ya just hop on my back an' we'll slip in there past your folks again."

"But they won't be up this late. They'll be gone t' bed."

"That," said Crosley, "is somethin' else I forgot t' tell ya about." And he reached down and snapped the I-ain't-here doodad off his belt and another whatchamacallit with it.

"Ya see this little dingus here?"

He handed it to me, and it looked just like a tiny telescope.

"Lissen to it," he said.

I held it to my ear, and I could hear this tiny ticking! The thing ticked like a little windup watch!

"That's right," said Crosley. "We're still gonna have t' sneak in there, cause when we left I pulled this time-spreader dingus all the way open, see here? An' ya know what happens when I do that —— ? It slows *time* way down all over your house! No foolin', buddy, when we get inside, it ain't gonna be more than a minute or two past your regular bedtime!"

We climbed up the stoop and peeked in through

the living room window. And he was right! Mom and Dad were still sitting there, and Dad still had his tennis magazine. But Mom had a book now instead of her crossword puzzle, and the cockeyed thing was, neither one of them *moved* at all. Their eyes were open and they seemed fine, but both of them looked as still as statues!

I watched and watched, and I thought maybe I saw Mom's hand starting to turn the page. But I don't know. If her hand did move, it moved like the hour hand on a clock!

Crosley opened the front door with the special skeleton key he had, and I got on his back and we crept inside.

"Squeeze the dingus all the way shut," whispered Crosley. "An' watch —— "

I did what he said, and as soon as I did I saw the page turn in Mom's book. And then Dad put down his magazine and yawned.

No kidding. My folks were moving around now just like always. But even if they turned and looked out in the hall, they wouldn't see Crosley and me sneaking by them because Crosley had the I-ain't-here doodad in his teeth.

Us Night Buddies snuck upstairs to my room and crept inside and left the door cracked open just enough to see. Crosley put the dingus away but kept the doodad out, and I started undressing.

"Hey lissen, buddy, your mom's gonna see them shoelaces in the mornin'."

"Hey, that's right." I took off the rest of my clothes. *"Ut!* Hey, I know what —— "

"Ut! yourself. What?"

"I'll just tell her Crosley got 'em for me in the all-night drugstore."

"Crosley who?" he grinned.

"Just plain Crosley," I said. I pulled my pajamas on and crawled in bed and felt my backside: "Cros—— "

"Yeah, chief?"

"Your back's as knotty as ever, Cros."

"Yerk! Yerk! Yerk! Yerk! Yerk!"

But you know what? I couldn't see him giggling now because he had gone ahead and stuck the doodad back in his teeth.

"Yerk! Yerk! Yerk! —— Lissen, I'll see ya real soon, man. Gonna sneak out now."

"I'll see you too, Crosley, right, Crosley?"

"Ya better believe it, ol' trouper! I'll be in the closet nextime, though, right?"

"Cool."

And then the bedroom door opened just a little bit wider ——

—— And Crosley wasn't there.

But that was okay. It really was. I was beat-down tired and I knew I wouldn't have any more trouble sleeping tonight. Or tomorrow night or the night after that either. I think my eyelids started drooping.

"EXCELSIOR!" I tried to say, but I'm not sure I got it all out.